CATHERINE MERRIMAN

Broken Glass

PAN BOOKS

First published 1998 by Pan Books
an imprint of Macmillan Publishers Ltd
25 Eccleston Place, London SW1W 9NF
and Basingstoke

Associated companies throughout the world

ISBN 0 330 35299 7

1 3 5 7 9 8 6 4 2

A CIP catalogue record for this book is available from
the British Library.

Typeset by SetSystems Ltd, Saffron Walden, Essex
Printed and bound in Great Britain by
Mackays of Chatham plc, Chatham, Kent

Chapter 1

Most of us have our cancers. Our personal, pet cancers. Nick's father, for instance – his personal cancers are cynicism and disrespect for the establishment. He blames David Frost and Mandy Rice-Davies. Seriously. David Frost for 1963's *That Was The Week That Was*, which in his view destroyed for ever the uncomplicated fifties innocence of the British public; and Mandy Rice-Davies for her 'Well, he would, wouldn't he?' of the same year, when Profumo declared himself guiltless of impropriety to his Honourable Friends. The cancer of cynicism and loss of innocence spawned at that time has since (Nick's father would say) spread unchecked, eating away at everything that is, or should be, decent and deserving of respect in society: the judiciary, the government, the royal family, even the professional classes. It's no good suggesting to him that these institutions have been revealed, through countless scandals or exposés, as unworthy of respect;

he would deny this (very politely, 'No, Jessica, let's be quite clear here') – it is merely individuals within the institutions that have let them down. If you confuse the two, and mock the institutions themselves, you undermine, you erode the essential structures of society. The body sickens and, eventually, dies. How much happier, healthier and well-ordered, he insists, society was in the fifties. I wouldn't know, not having been born until the next decade (around the time of *TW3*, actually) but it's always sounded a drab, naive decade to me.

My employer Francine's pet cancer is the gross commercialization of the world. The inexorable push towards Earth plc. It's what she's built her career on. Her malignant cells would be, I suppose, the multinational companies. Francine attempts, with my help, to frustrate their purpose, to protect or immunize the, as yet, uncontaminated parts of the world against their predations. At present the battleground is Eastern Europe, and the main enemies the agribusinesses and the nuclear energy industry. Whether multinationals can really be paralleled with cancer cells is a moot point; when industrial sectors are taken over they are not normally damaged beyond repair – though aspects of them may be. But they certainly mutate: change their nature and appearance, their purpose. Become satellites, octopus arms, feeding the corporate monster.

My cancer, I suppose, is apathy. An absence of care. Care-lessness. It's what I always come back to. Selfishness is another word for it, though that sounds too deliberately self-serving; selfishness is what it is in effect, not necessarily in purpose. I don't mind what people care about, as long as it's something besides themselves, and they don't separate their lives from their hearts. Flexing the care muscle is good for us. I don't know why, but I know it is. I suspect – because it involves imagination and empathy and abstract thought – it is what makes us human. Of course, you can't decide whether to care; one either does, or one doesn't. But the cancer is the spread of acceptance – the message, even – that it is all right not to care. That you yourself, even to the detriment of others, are all that matters, and all you are responsible for. When this cancer invades a formerly highly active organ – such as the young, for instance – the sickness can be particularly noticeable and painful to the whole. Francine complains that her children – these are the young I'm thinking of – have no concept of idealism. That they understand only materialism, romanticism, and hedonism. But even if lack of idealism is widespread – and her children are not, I would say, average young people – the cancer is a long way, still, from taking over the whole carcass. I am, anyway, an optimist, and believe in remissions. There are signs of one even now. But it is a shame people discovered that it is easy to do nothing; that no punishment descends on sideliners.

I don't think Nick has a personal, pet cancer like his father's, Francine's or mine. Not one he's definitely nailed his emotions to. He believes in freedom to do your own thing (or, more likely in his case, not do it) and bucks against petty rules, but I don't think he believes that a tendency to invent petty rules is sweeping like a cancer across the world. He despises junk-food culture but not, it has to be said, junk food. That would be hypocrisy indeed, from someone who a decade or so back, between the ages of eighteen and twenty-two, existed on little else.

So it is ironic that Nick, the only one among us to perceive no metaphorical cancers in society, should be the one to contract the real thing.

Tonight is Nick's first social engagement since his operation two months ago. We are going to the Playhouse and he still can't drive, so we're using my Golf. The invitation, which is to a fund-raising bash, was addressed to both of us, but sent to Nick. An act of economy, doubtless, but one which brings home to me the fact that I have spent more time at Nick's cottage recently than at my own flat. That physically, at least – in terms of strict propinquity – we have been drawn closer together.

We're in his cottage now, in the big low-ceilinged comfortable untidy living room. It's well named – apart from the kitchen and the lean-to conservatory out the back, this is the whole of the downstairs. There isn't a hall, even, or front-door lobby. The sitting part of the room is littered with Nick's essentials of life: Muriel, his acoustic guitar (so named because she is an Ovation and obviously female, all curves and belly), music and custom car magazines, and dozens of cushions. For himself, at the moment, or rather his leg, and his cat.

Nick is hovering by the front door, checking pockets in his jacket. It is late August. Warm enough not to wear a coat. Standing still, he looks normal. A little thin, but he's lost the alarming pallor that came from weeks behind hospital glass in high summer. His wound and dressings and swollen leg are hidden, and he can get his right foot into an ordinary shoe as long as he leaves the laces loose. His light summer jacket covers the drawstring top of his tracksuit-type trousers, which are still the only kind he finds comfortable. Especially if he's got to sit bent-legged in a car.

'OK?' He lifts his head from fussing with his jacket, and pushes his hair off his face. His hair hasn't been cut for three and a half months, because haircuts aren't something you think about in hospital, but he plans to deal with it next week. His hair is dark brown. A long time ago he used to dye it black. He is – or was – an expert on DIY hair dyes. His expression is sharp. Almost impatient.

'Ready,' I say, and clink the car keys at him. We go outside, and I have to remind him to lock the front door. Nick's cottage is a stone building with a white rendered frontage, standing in a small uninteresting garden – uninteresting only because Nick takes no interest in it. The virtues of the property, as far as he is concerned, are its large workshop garage at the back, where his own car is presently stored, and the cottage's distance from other properties. The freedom to make noise – music noise, that is – is vital to him.

I didn't bring the Golf in on to the hardstanding and it's parked in a layby a hundred yards down the lane. I'm aware that my progress towards it is even slower than Nick's. I'm more ambivalent about this outing. Nick will be meeting dozens of people he knows – I hesitate to call them friends – for the first time in months. He doesn't seem to be angry that none of them have visited him, either in hospital or at home, since he's been ill. Nor indeed, for the most part, even rung him. Or me.

I am angry. With them, and with Nick, for not, apparently, being angry. Men, I have been telling myself over the last couple of months, are hopeless friends. The hospital was a sixty-mile round trip away but Nick has been home for three weeks now and, apart from myself and Jason from the shop, no one has set foot in the cottage. Perhaps Nick never imagined otherwise. Perhaps he has other more fundamental things to worry about. It's I who displace my anger.

I climb into the driving seat of the Golf and we set off into town. The Playhouse is only half a mile the other side of the market town centre; we could have walked, just, if Nick had been fitter. As we pass the bronze War Memorial soldier outside the main Post Office I glance at Nick's face and am surprised by how positive he looks. He isn't normally a party person; not in anticipation, anyway, before he's got there and relaxed. I've dressed up for several parties he's pulled out of at the last minute. But of course this party is a first. A first of anything is a sign of progress. The life force is very strong in him at the moment – even when he's tired his eyes glint with it. He is pushing himself, always. Counting up the victories. Like when, two weeks ago, he first walked stickless to the end of his garden. All of thirty yards. Like when he made it to the layby a few days later, to meet me.

'Are you OK?' I ask, seeing him shift in the seat. There isn't a lot of room for a stiff leg in the Golf.

Nick gives a small nod and murmurs, 'Fine.' The briefest possible answer. For the last few hours he's been monosyllabic and I know why: he's conserving strength for the Playhouse. Even the scraps of energy that words take up deplete him at present. But, as if to make up for his shortness, he gives me a direct smile. He looks, yes, happy. I would pat him on the thigh, if it hadn't got a fresh, only recently healed six-inch scar on it.

'There's a cushion in the back,' I say. 'In case you get fed up with standing.' If Nick sits he's meant to put his leg up. I know that all the Playhouse chairs are hard plastic. His leg is still heavy and fluid-filled, and very sensitive to pressure.

We pull into the Playhouse entrance and I park in the Disabled Parking sector by the front door. Well,

Nick is, just at present, disabled. He's hardly limping, though, as we mount the steps. The Playhouse is an early nineteenth-century dressed-stone building which used to be the town workhouse; then was near-derelict for a hundred years, then renovated for small businesses, then converted to a municipal theatre and studios. The paintwork in the entrance foyer is a bilious council green. Gerry, who is an acquaintance rather than a friend, and chairman of Friends of the Playhouse, is taking tickets at the door.

'Nick and Jessica,' he announces, as if to some third party, though none is present. His red hair makes a woolly halo around his pink face. If I had hair like his I'd definitely shave my head. He beams. 'Great. How are you?'

'Not dead yet,' Nick says cheerfully.

Gerry is taken aback by this. I'm not sure he knows Nick has been ill. His smile is lopsided. His eyes flick at me.

'Nor me,' I say. Poor Gerry. He'll have to ask someone else. The 'How are you?' question from people who don't know is unanswerable at the moment. 'Ah, got cancer at the moment, old man. But it's coming along. I hope.' It won't work. The huge black baggage of it makes it impossible.

We are approaching the swing double doors. A girding-up moment, I feel. We have to enter a large room full of people, many of whom will know us. Nick runs the band practice room in the Playhouse. He hires or lends instruments and equipment. Plays himself in practice sessions, if the groups are short of a guitarist. Even on gigs, very occasionally. Nick is a musician and eleven years ago he was almost famous. Round here, in a nudging, provincial way, he still is.

I push through the doors. There are about sixty people inside, talking noisily. The walls are covered with theatre posters and black and white photographs. Nick features on several. The sound is befuddlingly loud – theatre staff and their supporters in full party cry. My eyes refuse to catch anyone's. I'm making for the bar. I don't look behind to see if Nick's following. Two female voices say, 'Hi Jess!' to me as I pass and I hear myself replying, 'Hi, hi,' without registering who is speaking. I am aware of two objectives: to get the physical bulk of the bar behind me, so I'm not adrift in this crowd, and to get enough space between myself and Nick to show that he is fit enough not to need an escort fluttering around him.

I smile at an elderly man who clearly recognizes me and say 'Hi!' again to another couple. Then I'm at the bar. Volunteers are serving and the choices are wine, beer or soft drinks. I buy a red wine for Nick, because I know the white won't be cold, and a tonic water for myself. Finally, a glass in each hand, I turn round.

Nick is some way behind me. He has been waylaid by Brian, the Playhouse manager. Good. That is what I had hoped for, by forging ahead. They'll have practicalities – when Nick might return to work, for instance – to talk about.

A voice in my right ear says, quietly and breathily, 'Jess?'

I swing round. It's Fay. Fay by name, fey by nature. Her pale-blue, doll-lashed eyes blink at me. Her expression is empathetic, tragic, insupportable.

'How is he?' she murmurs. 'I was so shocked when I heard. Well . . . we all were . . .'

We have known Fay and her partner Alan for many years. We may not know them much longer. For a moment I can't speak. I see an image of Nick and myself, alone, pariahs, untouchables, at the fringe of a crowd of shocked, breast-beating empathizers. Who are all these 'we's' for Christ's sake? I imagine hitting Fay. Punching her, very hard, on the delicate, pointed tip of her chin.

But I'm holding a glass in each hand. I say, possibly even with a smile, 'He's going to be fine. The consultant says he's delighted.' I'm breezy. It's nothing. What a fuss other people make.

'Wonderful.' Fay's voice tails off. She is staring at Nick. I can't help doing so too. It is cruel to see him against this robust, noisy company. An organ in my lower chest contracts, squeezing a droplet of terror into my veins. At the cottage I have grown used to his appearance.

'He's thin because he ran a fever for a month,' I say.

'He had a serious wound infection. It's nothing to do with the cancer.'

This is true. But I know what other people will think. Denial, poor girl. When people hear 'cancer', they expect thinness. When they see thinness, they wonder 'cancer?'. But Nick's hasn't spread. So far. The doctors have checked the melanoma site, his lymph glands, his lungs, his blood. So far, not a trace. There is an 'excellent' chance, the consultant told Nick, that there will be no recurrence. Of course, no one explains precisely what 'excellent' means.

'The shop,' says Fay. She has turned from looking at Nick, but her eyes are still pitying. 'How've you been managing?'

By 'you' she means Nick. His music shop is nothing to do with me.

'Jason's been keeping it ticking over.' Ah, I spot the boy now, the other side of the room. I put Nick's wine glass down and wave. With his long black hair tied loosely half-way down his back, he's looking particularly earringed and gipsyish. He's with a couple of male youth drama members and Brian's tall blonde teenage daughter. She's several inches taller than he is but I don't suppose this will worry him. Nothing much does. Jason is nineteen, only fourteen years younger than Nick and myself, but it feels like centuries. He believes everything we tell him, which is touching and immensely reassuring. Yes, Nick has cancer. But only skin cancer, you know, President Reagan had it on his nose, didn't kill him, did it? Jason doesn't know that there are different types. That some are very much more dangerous than others. That Nick's cancer, left untreated, would spread not across the surface of his skin, as the less dangerous cancers – at least initially – do, but deep into the organs of his body. And as Jason hero-worships Nick, and can't imagine anything bad about him, all he wants to hear is that he'll be fine, gonna walk it, no problem. Nick is frail now because of the wound infection, not the cancer. Well, it's true, isn't it? I wish I were nineteen.

It doesn't look as if Nick is going to break away from Brian for a moment or two, so I leave his glass where it is. Fay wants to move on, and as she murmurs, 'Bye, Jess, all the best,' she gives my forearm a squeeze of such compassion that I really do have to stop myself lashing out at her. At present the desire to hit things that offend me is very close to the surface.

Then a hand taps me on the shoulder. I turn, and it's Grace. I actually have to stop myself moaning, 'Oh, Grace.' I didn't expect to see her here; she's been working in Spain all summer. Her hair, usually a soft mouse colour, has bleached to a wheatstraw gold. Her skin glows with sun. Her smile is letterbox wide.

'The day before yesterday.' She's anticipated my question. 'And everyone's told me. You must have had a hell of a summer.'

How can I deny it? When it's handed to me, free,

like that? It's so hard to say, but so easy to agree with. What a relief.

'They're all scared of you, you know.' Grace's eyes sweep the company. Her mouth becomes mischievous. 'Even more than they usually are.'

'Shut up,' I say. I have a reputation for being pugnacious but it's completely undeserved.

She moves in close. 'What does it look like, Jess? I'm covered in moles.'

'Like a purple match-head. Growing out from a flat mole. Nick's was right on the edge of one.' I'm parroting this. The details are correct, but the fact is that I have no memory of Nick's tumour. I can't visualize it at all. Nick says that I first pointed it out to him; but I can't remember that, either. I'm happy to take the credit but feel mildly fraudulent, with no memory to back it. Presumably there are reasons why our minds erase things. I have only the dimmest memory of him telling me that it was cancer too, after returning from hospital outpatients. Naming the diagnosis that was impossible, that had never seriously crossed our minds. All I see is this picture, which includes me, as if my eyes have left my body. Me at my desk at work, vague above the shoulders, except for the dark cap that is my hair, and the black smudges beneath that are my wide-open eyes. Nick is flopped on the spare chair by the door, looking completely punctured, staring at nothing in particular. In my mind the scene is noisy, but of course it wasn't. That's just the sound shock makes in your head. Really it was pin-drop quiet.

Grace is looking over to Nick. I repeat myself. 'He's thin because he had a wound infection. They had to operate again to drain it. He was feverish for several weeks. He's putting on weight now.'

This isn't actually true but he's not losing it, anyway. He just hasn't got his appetite back yet.

'Die for those cheekbones,' says Grace, and then gives an appalled guffaw.

I laugh too. We need more tasteless, reckless jokes. They're the ones that make you feel safe, normal. Grace is well known for her big mouth, metaphorical as well as literal. She once told me on the short train journey to Bristol that she and her boyfriend were going to a jumble sale the next day, with the sole intent of buying clothes that they could rip off each other. They acquired new wardrobes, she said, most weekends. She has a loud voice and as we disembarked from the train two helpful men told her that they had jumble sales in Bristol too, very good ones, every day.

Grace says, 'He's not going to die, is he?'

'No. Most don't.' I manage to say this confidently. In my head I hold two percentage figures: sixty and forty. I have convinced myself that the sixty per cent is the survival figure. Not the forty. The statistics are similar, I know, to those for breast cancer in women. However this is all information I acquired before Nick was ill, and I can't check it now. I can't read anything about the subject at all. Call it the blind-terror syndrome. But I do know that, overall, most young people with cancer (young meaning under forty) do not, these days, die from it. Kids, especially, don't. I know this is true because I heard it on the radio just the other day, while striding across the room to switch the set off.

Nick has finished his conversation with Brian and joins us. Grace says, 'Nick,' and embraces him in her usual manner, a kind of hanging neck lock, though she is perhaps more gentle with him than normal. She kisses his cheek and releases him. I give him his wine.

'On the thigh, was it?' Grace asks, as casually as if it hasn't been three months since she last saw him. 'Don't have much luck with that leg, do you. Isn't that the one you electrocuted?'

Nick and I look at each other. She's right. Not that I knew Nick in those days – neither did Grace – but everyone knows the story. How Nick was playing an open-air concert in Manila and someone hadn't checked the electrical earthing, so that when the neck of his guitar clipped a microphone both became live and he was thrown from the stage. He was lucky to escape with concussion and a burned thigh, where the guitar socket cable melted against him. If the accident had happened at the beginning of the tour he would probably have been treated in a local hospital, and caught the others up after a few days; as it was the tour was all but over, the insurance was up to date, and the record company couldn't resist the publicity bonus of alarmist announcements and an air-ambulance trip home. His picture made all the newspapers. And maybe they were right to make a drama out of it, because, as it turned out, the accident was the climactic end to his rock career; within six months he and the group had parted.

'D'you think . . . ?' I say. Could there be a connection? I'd forgotten about the burn. You can hardly see the scar, these days. It certainly isn't where the cancer started. But it must have traumatized the leg . . .

Nick shrugs and says, 'Who cares?' I start to argue, but stop myself. Of course he's right. It's a masochist's game, asking yourself why. Why cancer? Why me? Or looking for cause and effect. Your brain asks these questions – you can't stop it – but lingering on them is futile. Thereby lies the pointless pain of self-recrimination. No one, whatever their lifestyle, deserves cancer. And risk factors are merely that: factors that can predispose. The people most likely to develop malignant melanoma, we're told every summer, are fair-haired, blue-eyed, pale-skinned office workers who toast themselves once a year in hot foreign suns. Nick is dark-haired and brown-eyed and his skin tans without him bothering to sunbathe. He doesn't wear shorts, has never sunburned his thighs (as far as he can remember) and has not been abroad for more than a decade. So much for risk factors.

So much for our first post-op social engagement too. I've loved seeing Grace and we've only been here twenty minutes, but my legs have started to shake. I fight the stress mentally, that's the trouble, so it comes out physically. I let Nick push across the room to have a quick word with Jason – though they speak on the phone most days about work – and then join them after a few minutes and say I'm tired, and want to go home. I don't say that Nick also looks tired, though he does. He looks satisfied, too – another notch on the normality belt – but at the moment half an hour on his feet, especially just standing, not going anywhere, is his limit. I daren't wait until he's really had enough. The day after he came out of hospital he spent far too long checking over his guitars in the living room and when he tried to get back upstairs he nearly didn't make it. I spotted him three quarters of the way up, hanging on to the banister with his head down as if he were going to faint. I rushed up behind him and pushed him up the last few steps and he said, 'OK, OK,' testily, as if he'd just been having a rest and I was overreacting, but I don't think I was.

We say our farewells and it seems to me that more people are prepared to cry, 'Goodbye!' at us, and with more enthusiasm, than were prepared to cry, 'Hello!' But this may be just my imagination. A function of my mood. Outside the hall Nick's shoulders sag and he starts to walk like a man whose motor is running down.

Back at the cottage he looks punched out around the eyes. It's after nine-thirty and anyone else who looked as rough would be allowed to totter straight to bed, but he doesn't have that luxury. There's a ritual to perform first. This is why Nick mustn't get too tired. He's got a serious wound to deal with before bedtime.

We've got the performance down to half an hour now. When he first came home and was so frighteningly slow it took more than an hour. The routine's this: he runs a bath upstairs and throws a handful of salt into it. Then he undresses and removes the elastic footless stocking off his right leg. He inspects the cancer site, which is now just a neat six-inch pink line running up the front of his thigh. The stitches dissolved weeks ago. Then he untapes the large dressing low down on the right of his abdomen, throws it away, and removes a thin pink latex wedge, about seven inches long, from the open gash of the wound. This wound is where the surgeons went in to find the blood supply to his leg, so they could treat just the limb – with chemicals that included a radioactive isotope – and not poison the rest of him. It's also where they removed some of his lymph glands. This is the wound that became infected, and this is why it is being healed open. They daren't risk another abscess and, anyway, the tissue is damaged: stitches wouldn't hold. This kind of healing takes a long time. To begin with the wound was eight inches long and two deep, but it's been granulating steadily in from the sides. Each week the hospital makes a new foam bung by squirting liquid latex in and letting it set. Each week the pink slug is shorter and thinner. The wound doesn't hurt at all. The nerve endings round the incision gave up a long time ago.

But the bung has to be removed each morning and evening to be disinfected, while Nick soaks the wound in warm salty water. I bring up a foil tray and the brown bottle of Hibitane disinfectant, which is normally kept in the fridge. Nick deals with everything himself now – the bung removal, cleaning, and replacement. I just fetch and carry. For someone who is squeamish about even fake television gore, Nick has come a long way. In the evenings I take up a half tumbler of dark rum too, for him to drink in the bath. He's not a rum drinker when we're out, or even downstairs, but it has something to do with the water, he says, and the survival of revolting physical ordeals. I make sure he doesn't have access to the whole bottle. Twice in the last three weeks the wound's been treated to a rum-and-salt-water wash, because Nick's fallen asleep with the bottle across his chest. I don't imagine it did the wound any harm, but it's a waste of good alcohol.

Tonight I have a nip myself downstairs and watch the beginning of the television news. I have to lie on a mountain of cushions and magazines on the sofa, but Nick's old ginger cat and I don't mind. Toby's getting bony too, like his master. His purr suggests the liquid rumble of an inboard boat engine, and is the most soothing sound in the world.

When I hear the floorboards creak above me, and

the click of the bedroom door, I put the cat aside and walk up. The bath water is still gurgling down the plug hole in the bathroom. I put the dressing packs and micropore tape back in the wall cupboard and remove the Hibitane and place it on the small table out on the landing, so I won't forget to take it down to the fridge. Then I go through to the bedroom.

Nick is already in bed. He has to lie either on his back, or on his good side, turned away from the door. Only the small bedside lamp is on. I sit down next to his back and put my hand on his head. You can tell a lot from heads. They react to illness. Hair does, especially. Nick's hair feels clean and unclumped, and is damp at the ends. Still thick. I'm grateful he didn't lose it. His right leg remains smooth and naked, though the doctors promise the hair'll grow again.

'Why don't you purr too?' I ask.

Nick turns his head and his face cracks into a smile. He's exhausted, and his eyes are dark pits, but he's doing his best. As if he understands that even with me – perhaps especially with me – he must never give up.

'Went OK tonight, didn't it?'

'They don't deserve you.'

There's a short silence before Nick says, 'You staying?'

I mull it over, and then say, 'I don't think so.' I don't sleep well beside Nick at the moment. His leg is too swollen and tender and encroaching. He still groans a lot. And he grabs hold of me in his sleep. It's touching and sometimes even arousing, but it doesn't get me rested. It's vital that one of us is fit. I have a terror of being ill too, of not being able to cope.

Nick says, 'The shop only took seventy quid last week.'

I sigh. I'm glad Jason doesn't grasp the danger Nick is in and the stress he's under, but it also means he doesn't understand about protecting him.

'The stock's low, that's all. And there'll be the school rentals in a couple of weeks.'

'Suppose Jason leaves? I'll have to write him a top-up cheque tomorrow.'

Jason's been drawing his own wages out of takings. He's completely trustworthy.

'Jason would work for you for nothing,' I remind Nick. 'Jason thinks he has the best job in the universe. Jason thinks you're ace, man.'

Nick smiles. I smile too. I'm not seriously worried about the music shop. You have to have priorities. Nick could survive without shop income for a while. He's a lucky man; not many make their megabucks, and retain a remnant to cushion them all their lives if they're careful, when they're scarcely more than boys. This is what Nick did; between the ages of eighteen and twenty-two, when he was blasted off that stage, he made a small fortune and, thanks mostly to his father who refused to be dazzled or steam-rollered by the music industry and knew his son was still a kid, kept a fair portion of it. Of the four of them in the original group Nick has probably come off best. The drummer is still working – and well-thought of – but could never hang on to his cash and has been bankrupted twice. The bass player is an alcoholic and on social security. The singer-keyboard player is seriously rich in Hollywood, writing film scripts now rather than song lyrics, but he is also seriously deaf. Nick left the group several years before it finally imploded and still needs to work, but not as hard as most people, and because he co-wrote several of the group's more popular songs he even gets royalty cheques from time to time. And his hearing remains excellent.

I take Nick's temperature – another nightly ritual as long as his wound remains open – then kiss him goodnight and go home. Home is back to the centre of town, to my small flat above Arnolds the newsagents, and, more importantly, opposite Batemans, the master bakers. Never mind the exotic breads they sell; Batemans is the home of the custard cream, fudge cake and ginger horn, the almond slice, Viennese finger, cream doughnut and madeleine. I didn't buy this flat because of where it was located, but I'd think twice about moving. I have a sweet tooth – no, a cake tooth – and never, ever, lose my appetite.

The flat feels chilly inside the front door and has a dusty, neglected air to it. Not surprising; it has been neglected, and undusted, over the last two months. There's one message on my answerphone and I know without listening to it that it's from my mother. I know the message too – or at least, the subtext of it. That Nick is going to die, that cancer is catching and that I should get out of the relationship before it kills me too. She doesn't say this, but she offers escape routes, and behind them I hear what sounds like panic, a desire to distance herself – and me – from catastrophe. I hate her at the moment, for having no faith in either of us. I'll ring her back tomorrow.

I sit down for a moment in front of my blank television screen. I thought I was tired and I am, but it's more a tense tiredness than a sleepy one. I need my own cat. Since I haven't got one, I go into the bedroom, change my skirt for leggings, and put on my training shoes. I'll go running.

Night running. You can do it in a town like this. A long time ago I lived in London and I did it there too, until anxiety stopped me. Other people's anxiety; nothing unpleasant ever happened to me, but once I caught the fear there was no point. Running is meant to be a relaxation, not an ordeal. I gave up. Then I had a year of asthma attacks, and I moved here. And now I run again, and have stopped worrying, and my lungs haven't seized on me once.

Tonight I run my usual route. How boring, people say, to have a habitual route, but they miss the point. Running is not about where you go or what you see. Where you go is inside your head, and what you see is a new perspective. The running must be routine, mentally unstimulating, to achieve this. To loosen body and mind. The biology of running is easy: it's the biology of any exercise that produces endorphins, the morphine of the mind. Dancing will do it. Aerobics will do it. But running you can do on your own, day or night, without music, equipment or home space. You need only two attributes for running, both of which I've got: small breasts, because otherwise it's uncomfortable, and hair that's no fuss to wash, because you get sweaty. My hair's short enough to wash and towel dry in five minutes. Beyond that, anyone can run. And when you do it regularly you're rewarded with a body that works properly and looks slim and fit, and which can accommodate as many cream cakes as you ask of it.

I run twice round the outside of the town park (because the gates are locked this time of night) then down a residential road to the river and back along a path through the river fields. The path's not lit but there's a bright white half-moon tonight and I'm not alone. Several people are giving their dogs bedtime walks and there's more a sense of silent camaraderie among us than of mutual risktaking.

It has taken a while for my mind to loosen. Now, on the home straight, I wonder how it is that you can be surer than you've ever been that you love someone and want them and care about them, but at the same time feel cut off from them more than ever before. This is how it is between Nick and myself. Cancer is a true enemy. Its tactics are divide and rule. Only one of us has his cancer. We are no longer an equal couple. The ground we were standing on split, as it shifted beneath us. We are forced into separate roles. Labelled differently. Patient, carer. Victim, non-victim. The vulnerable, the strong.

The wall between us is glass and, when pushed, can wrap very close around him. But it is still cold to the touch. He has the cancer, and I do not.

Chapter 2

Nick looked better after six hours of surgery than I had expected. They hadn't put any clothes on him but bare skin somehow looks healthier than new, unfamiliar pyjamas. He didn't seem to be in any pain. He seemed more worried by the hard nozzle of the drip connection in the back of his hand than by the wounds in his thigh and abdomen. A nurse took the nozzle out while I was there.

Something was wrong with the air in the hospital. Nick said he felt muzzy, and no wonder. It was dead and thick and seemed to make breathing difficult. Like invisible, energy-sucking fog. It attacked me the moment I entered the building; just walking through the main shop-lined concourse on the ground floor I could feel power draining from me. Up on the ward I sat beside Nick's bed and read day-old issues of the *Guardian*, the *Star*, the *Mirror* and *The Times* while he dozed. When he surfaced I remembered to tell him that his father had phoned, and hoped to be down as soon as his chest infection had cleared, and that his sister sent her love all the way from Canada. It was a quiet visit. I drove back to the cottage and fed Toby, and rang Paul – Nick's father – and told him Nick was fine. Then I rang my mother and said the same thing. I said I was fine too. I stayed over on my own in the cottage for the second night running.

The next day Nick was grumpy. He was starting to feel uncomfortable; they'd had to give him sleeping pills overnight. He complained that I talked too fast. I do talk fast. Especially when I'm stressed. I can't help it.

This was the day I read the notes at the bottom of his bed and discovered that the title given to his operation was not, as we had thought, a 'lymph' profusion, but a 'limb' profusion. I felt dizzy. It seemed a huge misapprehension. Not, I told myself, that it made any difference. It simply meant that they were profusing his leg via his vascular, rather than lymph, system. Obviously. How could I have thought otherwise? Why couldn't they have called it a 'leg' profusion? What else had we got wrong?

I noticed the other patients in the room that day. The young man in the bed on Nick's right spent the entire visiting session snogging his girlfriend in a whole-body clinch. On the bed. Without drawing the curtains. Nick whispered to me that he was an actor, 'resting' at the moment, and had confessed to a nightmarish week before admission. He'd had a bust-up with his girlfriend, appalling piles, and finally a prolapse of his rectum. However a collapsing bum seemed just the thing to retrieve lost girlfriends – I assumed this was the same one. She was actually rather an attractive, intelligent-looking woman, when she didn't have her tongue wedged in her boyfriend's mouth. He'd have been handsome if he hadn't had one of those noses that look permanently assailed by foul odours.

Opposite was a man about Nick's age called Gareth. He had stones in his bile duct and was bright yellow. Nick told me that, the night before, the nurses had shaved his midriff for his operation and because he was extremely hairy and a dark Celt, he'd ended up looking like a dozy wasp.

Part of Nick's discomfort came from the elastic bandage they had now wrapped round his leg. Sister had warned him to expect a lot of swelling. It looked to me as if this had started already. The bandage was wound from ankle to groin, and kept unravelling, most irritatingly. Nick was still very tired. I only stayed an hour. I returned straight to work in my office in Francine's house and remained there late, so I wouldn't have a long evening to myself. I could do any work-hours I liked because Francine was on holiday in Italy for a month. I'd given Toby a double helping of cat food before I left for the hospital, so I didn't bother to call in at the cottage again till the next morning.

When I visited Nick that afternoon I found him in

homicidal mood. He ordered me to bring in a sawn-off shotgun next visit, and a paper and pen so he could draw up a death list. He smiled as he said it, but his eyes were black and quite without humour. I don't think of him as a man with grievances, but they were oozing up from way back. Top of the list was his old school head of music, the man who made his life hell when he dropped cello and took up guitar. Who told him that he was an ungrateful musical hooligan unworthy of the school's attention, causing problems with his poor confused parents for more than a year. (Who, till then, had understood that they were harbouring a musical genius.) Then came the two boys who stole and trashed his old Jag just after he'd finished restoring it, and then the doctor who broke the news of his mother's fatal heart attack to his father in front of a room full of emergency patients. And lastly the man from Data-Met who sold him that crap computer printer for the shop for twice what it would have cost mail order.

The list almost convinced me that Nick had had a hard life; but of course he hasn't. Everyone, in a murderous enough mood, could write their own death list.

When the drugs trolley came round, in the middle of the visit, Nick asked the nurse for a Brompton cocktail, which didn't amuse her. A Brompton cocktail is heroin in alcohol, a medication devised to make dying more comfortable. The nurse looked even more reproving when he said, 'Got something for girlfriends, then, have you?' My expression – I was making a real effort to speak slowly and quietly – prompted him to add, 'Just a joke,' rather ungraciously. I was aware then, for the first time, of some fundamental shift in our relationship. That I was going to have to make allowances for someone I'd never given an inch to before. I didn't like the feeling.

He asked me to bring in some Satriani tapes and a Walkman next time, along with the shotgun. The only channel he could get through the hospital headphones was some lonely sounding female desperate for hospital requests. He said I could put her on the death list too, if I wanted.

Gareth also seemed in a depressed mood. He looked rocky after his operation. It was a complete success, but the consultant had advised him against putting the removed gallstones in his tropical fish tank, which was what he had been planning, in case they poisoned the fish. Gareth's disappointment seemed out of all proportion to the news. I stayed until supper time, then went home and fed Toby before returning to my flat. There were messages waiting for me from Paul, my mother, and Jason. I rang all three. Only Jason heard about the shotgun, because I knew he'd think it was funny, and not understand how worrying it really was.

The next day I arrived on the ward to find Nick being set up for a blood transfusion. I had ten minutes of deep panic until I found Sister who explained that he needed it because he was seriously anaemic and the chemicals they'd swamped his leg with had killed off red cells as well as cancer cells. The transfusion, she assured me, was almost routine. She said it would stop him feeling so low and tired – and murderous too, she might have added, though she didn't. When her words finally sank in, I was relieved. She was saying that there might be a physical reason for his depressed spirits. (Not the knowledge that he'd got cancer, and needed radical treatment for it, and might still die of it, oh no.)

But despite their insistence that they were just about to set the transfusion up they didn't, while I was there, anyway. Nick grumbled that no one should be allowed to qualify in medicine until they'd spent a period as an inpatient, so that they'd have some idea of what it was like to be on the receiving end of waffle, fudged replies, sudden major decisions, and things that were supposedly going to happen immediately not happening for hours. And he complained that no one made allowance for the fact that patients were unwell, and liked information delivered slowly, directly, and repeated, if possible.

However the transfusion was done soon after I left that day, and Sister was right; the next day Nick was dramatically improved. When I arrived in the late afternoon he greeted me with a robust, 'Hi!' and told me that he and Gareth had even started watching the film *The Stud* the night before in the day room – only hours after the transfusion – though they'd given up after twenty minutes, exhausted by the disco dancing.

Both men were in cheerfully aggressive mood. All three in the room (the fourth bed was empty) wore only their pyjama trousers – though Nick could only just get his on over his infuriating unravelling bandage – and both Nick and Gareth had bandages on their torsos; because they were all youngish men there was a definite field hospital look to the room. The actor even had a pile of beer cans on his bedside locker, which he was encouraging everyone to sample.

I wouldn't have wanted Nick in this mood all the time, and I pitied the nurses having to deal with such bolshie vulnerable men, but I didn't mind it just for now. Nick is seldom laddish at home and I didn't mind being reminded of his masculinity and how different and separate he is from me. It was a comfort, almost; like the pleasure I get from his musical gifts. The glorious sense that they have nothing to do with me, are beyond my influence or control, and are simply a free incomprehensible bonus in our relationship. I went home much less upset than I had arrived, and at the cottage told Toby not to worry, that his master was going to be all right. Then I went for a long celebratory run.

The next day we had an appointment booked with Nick's consultant to discuss worries we might have and I came into the hospital in the late morning especially for it. But on arrival I was told that there had been a medical emergency elsewhere and the consultant couldn't make it, sorry. I had yet to come across a doctor in the hospital, though of course Nick saw one every day – or rather, saw about a dozen, since the consultant was always accompanied by a gaggle of students, the hospital being a teaching institution. The only doctor he could talk to one-to-one was the houseman, but this wasn't a lot of help, since he referred all queries to the consultant, whom Nick had never seen without his entourage. There was a long list of questions I wanted answers to: what, exactly, had they done to Nick's leg? Why was it so huge? How long would it take to recover? Why didn't anyone explain what was happening? But every time I raised the questions with Nick he looked harassed, as if I was blaming him for not asking them himself, or remembering the consultant's answers to them, so I couldn't push it.

Two good things did happen that day, though. Nick's unravelling bandage was replaced by a much more comfortable stretch toe-less stocking, and a date was set for his discharge. Assuming someone would undertake to care for him at home (that meant me) he could leave in forty-eight hours.

Gareth opposite was hardly yellow at all by now, and was going home that afternoon. He still didn't look well; but then, hospital, unless you actively need treatment, isn't a safe place to linger in.

I went home after lunch, did half a day's work, and back at the flat made a list of all the jobs to be done the next day, to be ready for Nick's discharge. Changing the sheets on his bed. Getting food in for him; things like that.

But when the next day came the hospital wrong-footed us: minutes before I was about to leave work to visit Nick he rang to say that the consultant had just done his ward round, and told him he was free to go. This was somehow so typical of the hospital – to tell us something that sounded completely definite one day, and within twenty-four hours alter it – that I felt we should have outguessed them. But of course I was delighted. Never mind that I hadn't prepared the cottage, got the food in, or bought Toby his party hat.

I brought Nick home. Sitting in his own chair in his own living room for the first time in eight days he looked touchingly happy. Exhausted, but happy. His leg was huge and so tender he could scarcely walk, he had long incision lines in his thigh and abdomen, he was pumped full of someone else's blood, but all the tests he'd had had been clear, the consultant claimed he was pleased, and he'd survived. He scooped up Muriel and picked out the first chords of his old group's biggest hit song: 'Lords of the Universe'. I clocked him with a copy of *Custom Car*. Then I rang his father, his GP and finally Jason, to tell him Nick was on the phone again, but that I'd personally disembowel him if he rang about anything to do with work. I made Nick supper, changed the sheets on his bed, and stayed over.

And the next morning, would you believe, we had

sex. That's exactly what it was: no more, no less. Very cautious, very careful, very unabandoned, but absolutely successful sex. And afterwards, in the triumphant, life-affirming glow of it, told ourselves, very stupidly, but maybe understandably, that it was all over.

It is now the first of October, a month after our visit to the Playhouse, and I'm at work in Francine's house. Francine Brackenbury lives in a yellow-stone farmhouse with a red pantiled roof, detached from the land it once had, but with a two-acre shrub-and-lawned garden, about a mile out of town. It is approached from a lane that starts in a council estate and fizzles out in border-county hills, in genteel, moneyed Range Rover territory. Francine's house is geographically and socially part of the latter.

I am giving Francine two items of good news: first, that Nick's abdomen is now bungless, his wound completely healed, and second, that his leg is now strong enough for him to drive safely, so his ancient car is back on the road.

Francine says, 'Wonderful, Jess!', which might sound a platitude from anyone else, but doesn't from her. Francine is always sincere. Her favourite positives are 'wonderful', 'blissful' and 'heavenly', and the negatives are 'nightmare', 'insane' and 'ghastly'. I love hearing her say any of them; she sounds so ringingly upper class, so sweepingly, unarguably right.

I say I'm at work and I am, but physically we're in her rustic Italian-tiled kitchen, so she can give me work instructions while she cooks for a dinner party she's hosting tonight. She's making a vegetable terrine and at this precise moment is lining the terrine dish with spears of blanched asparagus. Her silver-blonde hair is tied back inelegantly with a horsy headscarf and her face is shiny and without make-up; none the less, at forty-six Francine is still, in a classy, unstrived-for way, a beautiful woman. She was once a society belle and featured in magazines like the *Tatler*. That was before she married Lionel, and caught the green bug.

I'm sitting at her pitch-pine kitchen table, pen and various papers in hand. Francine is giving me an update on responses to our latest environmental appeal – support for organic farming projects in the Czech Republic and Poland. Her voice is huskier than usual; she's only recently back from Eastern Europe and has a touch of Prague throat caused by air pollution from the brown sulphurous coal the power stations burn there. This is what our organization, known as Demeter, does: we transfer funds from Western sponsors to East European environmental causes. We have other projects, but at present that's the bulk of it. We invite projects, offer assistance in formulating prospectuses, and then canvass organizations and individuals here. We initiate and facilitate. Francine knows an enormous number of people: people in the environmental movement, people running charitable trusts, people in the establishment, and, most importantly, people with money. This is her husband Lionel's legacy. Lionel is no longer involved in Demeter, since green matters stopped being cutting edge and sexy but, from the days when he was – a principled sideline to his other, more lucrative, business activities – he has delivered to Francine bulging address books of contacts. Luckily for us – and our East European counterparts – most are not as fickle as he. The driving idea behind all this – a David and Goliath notion, if ever there was – is to get in before the multinationals take over. Or, more realistically, to make sure that there is a vocal and properly funded opposition to their predations. Agriculture and power generation are areas particularly in our sights. We – the Demeter office – are ourselves funded by a loyal couple of thousand subscribing members, mostly British, who in return for occasional newsletters donate at least fifteen pounds each a year to our running costs. Many give considerably more.

Despite the ambitiousness of our aims, and the politics that is necessarily involved, Francine is not, paradoxically, a very political person. If she were, she might make more connections. She might not, perhaps, send her children to public school, which she does (or did, in Celia's case) and, being a vegetarian, might not support fox hunting, which she also does. She is a country person and believes in country pursuits, though these do not include intensive farming practices or diversification into caravan parks. She and I do not discuss politics except where it directly impinges on environmental matters in hand. Francine is friendly with both Tories and Socialists, and moves in circles where she is likely to know more of the former. She is a rural lady, passionate about Nature, and uninterested in taking anything to its crude political – especially party political – conclusion. She trusts environmental arguments even when she has forgotten their actual substance. Anyway, she doesn't need logical argument; she's knows, intuitively, that what she does is right. Which it is. We're tiny fry, of course, compared to the environmental big fish, but small is still beautiful in the green world, and there's room – and scope – for everyone.

'Lord Packham's secretary rang last night,' Francine says. 'He's good for four thousand. Dear Peter.' She smiles fondly. 'But he must have the leaflet material we funded for Poland to show to the trustees. Can you put them on the list?'

'Right.' I pull out my pink distribution list. As usual my eyes catch the top two names on the first page, which in my pleasure at entering, I boldly underlined. The Museum of Peace and Solidarity in the Ukraine, and the Victoria and Albert Museum in London. Both collect campaigning material. Both have curators who write using first names. Dimitri from the Ukraine even sends me picture postcards if I haven't been in touch for a while, saying, 'Hi? No leaflets? For us?'

I add Lord Packham's trustees to the list and then

get up to return to my office, but Francine cries, 'No, have lunch first,' waving a cupful of vegetable puree left over from filling the terrine dish. 'I'll make some toast.'

I sit down again. Unless Francine is out, or away, we always eat lunch together and, during lunch, we don't talk shop. We are more than employer and employee. Anyone watching us would probably assume we were friends. But we're not, though we are, certainly, friendly. Except by accident – because we live in a small town – we don't see each other outside work. She would not invite me to one of her dinner parties, any more than I would suggest a meal out together at the pub. We move in different social circles, and have different values. Francine, for instance, sees herself, since Lionel lost interest in their marriage and decamped to Oxford, as impoverished. But her kind of poverty is not a kind I'd recognize. She bought an urn for the garden last week for two hundred pounds. When I reminded her that just the day before she had claimed she was destitute, she protested, 'Oh yes, but, Jess, this is an investment!' Truly poor people, I feel, can't even afford investments. Nor do they have dinner parties for twelve. Nor do they share a London flat with their husband. Nor do they catch aeroplanes as if they were taxis. Nor do they tell everyone how ridiculously broke they are, and laugh about it. Nor do they direct a business as time-consuming as Demeter without drawing a penny beyond expenses from it.

While Francine makes toast I boil a kettle on her Aga and make myself a cup of coffee. Francine doesn't drink coffee. She is much more health conscious than I. We also, as environmentalists, have different dietary settling points. She is totally vegetarian. I merely avoid beef; not for health reasons – my view is that, unlike pigs and sheep (whose respective natural habitats are woodlands and uplands) beef cattle occupy land that could be used far more productively for vegetable crops. And beef ranches destroy forests. You could say – indeed, many do – that the beefburger culture ravages the world. But omitting beef is as far as I am prepared to restrict my diet. I have never confessed to Francine the extent of my cream-cake habit.

As we sit down at the table to eat Francine says, 'I was rather hoping Celia would be back from town by now.'

'Is she still here?' Francine's daughter Celia finished her first year at Nottingham University this summer. I'd assumed her second year had already started.

'Oh . . .' Francine shrugs. 'Didn't I tell you? She's not going back. Immediately, that is. She's taking a year off.'

'Goodness!' This is what I mean about us not being friends. I would have known, if we had been.

'Her bust up with that ghastly Jonathan. She doesn't feel strong enough to face him. He'll have gone by next year. She says she's emotionally exhausted.'

This is possible. Celia is a passionate person, like

her mother. She feels, oh, like no one can have possibly felt before. You get a sense of this with Francine too, but she redeems herself with her impeccable manners. However passionately Francine feels, she never loses sight of others. Celia is only nineteen, and sees only herself.

'I didn't realize they'd actually broken up,' I say. 'I mean, I knew there were problems . . .'

'Well, they have. Thank God. Thank God.'

I never met the ghastly Jonathan. I suspect that I would not find him as ghastly as Francine does. Francine is not a fan of very young adults, despite having two as children. She doesn't like the way they look today, whether they are dreadlocked crusties, preppy types reeking of aftershave, or floppy-haired students. She doesn't like the way they speak, their attitudes, the self-serving things they get up to. Her ideal young man would resemble a youthful Cary Grant – who must have been well into middle-age, surely, in Francine's own youth? – and would be clean, confident, sophisticated, self-deprecating, charming and knowledgeable and come from a good family. Francine makes no apology for feeling that her children should socialize within their own class. This has very little to do with snobbery, much more to do with a non-western desire to uphold traditions and standards, and match like, romantically, with like. Jonathan's ghastliness was, possibly, no more than a gross incompatibility with these ideals. I have seen one photo. He looks an untidy youth, with a pony tail and leather bracelet thongs around his wrists. Anathema to Francine: in addition she says he is dirty and has boorish table manners.

'What is she going to do all year?' I am really most surprised. It is not like Francine to let her children off anything. She must have felt very strongly about the issue, to contemplate the prospect of her daughter at a loose end for a year.

Francine shrugs. 'Develop a few skills, hopefully. I'm not having her doing nothing. Travel a bit, possibly, when she's feeling stronger. I thought . . .' she catches my eye, and I get the feeling she's making a quick mental amendment, '. . . computing. Or at least key-boarding. In the evenings, of course.'

'Good idea.' Francine is assuring me that I won't have to share the office with Celia. That's where the computer is. It's suddenly occurred to her that I wouldn't like it. Fat chance anyway; Celia's not going to be interested in office skills. She's a girl for exotica. T'ai chi, calligraphy, aromatherapy . . .

'Actually,' Francine says, wiping her hands carefully on a napkin, 'she says she'd like to learn a musical instrument.'

'Oh yes?'

'I wonder. Would Nick teach her the guitar?'

I feel an instant negative reaction to this, though it's hard to explain why. Perhaps because I have a negative feeling towards Celia generally. Public school kids – or, at least, Francine's public school kids – baffle me. They seem, in their attitudes and tastes, either astonishingly behind, or in front of, their comprehensive school peers. When Celia was fifteen, she was into the Beatles. As sadly unfashionable a taste – at that time – as one could imagine. Now, though, the Beatles are generally in favour again; but Celia, predictably, has moved on. On her bedroom wall – I know, because I've housesat for Francine – there is – or was, less than two years ago – a picture of Nick. Not on his own, of course. With his old group, at a time when they'd adopted a vaguely sinister neo-gothic look. Dyed black hair, a suggestion of eye-liner, flowing sepulchral evening wear. Apparently, ten years after everyone else had forgotten them, they'd become a minor cult at her school. It gave me a shock, seeing him on her wall. He's been an ordinary person living a quiet life as long as I've known him; I've tended to believe he belongs to me. And his face, in those days, was so blank and young. So unwritten on. It may be from that moment that I've mistrusted Celia.

'He does still do lessons, doesn't he?' Francine is asking.

'Oh, yes. Yes.' I mentally pull back. I'm not getting involved in this. It may well be Francine's idea. I have mentioned that the shop hasn't been doing well, with Nick's only limited presence. He still can't manage more than a few hours daily. Perhaps Francine thinks he could use the work. He charges eight pounds a half hour for guitar lessons.

'You can ring him at home,' I say. 'Any time. Or Celia can. Home or shop, he doesn't mind.'

Francine nods and says, 'Lionel is keen she do something too. He doesn't want her wasting a whole year. Obviously.'

No, I can imagine Lionel wouldn't. Even more than Francine, Lionel is a person of energy. An achiever. A successful, steam-rolling entrepreneur. In his time, an excellent provider. But also, as it has turned out, an opportunist, a blatant adulterer, and a deserter. Ah well, you can't have everything. Actually I've only met Lionel three times. I am, in a sense, his replacement at Demeter. Francine needed help after he left, so she employed me. He visits Francine and his children regularly but usually at weekends, when I'm not here. Nearly everything I know about him has come from Francine. She wouldn't lie, but her reports might be coloured.

I spend all afternoon sending letters and faxes to rich people, but with my mind on Celia. Stupid, but I can't help it. I recognize minor obsession, but it doesn't stop me obsessing. Nothing is solid or sacred any more; danger, I know now, can erupt anywhere. And Francine, I am sure, is blind about Celia. Like, in the early days, she was blind about Lionel. She has told me stories about him: once he forced her to babysit for one of his local mistresses, while he was actually out with the woman. To be fair to him, the crime wasn't planned; the lover's children panicked and rang the restaurant where they were eating after being abandoned by their teenage babysitter, and Lionel didn't want to spoil his evening, but clearly didn't mind the idea of ringing Francine and ruining hers. He presented the situation as an emergency – of course Francine went, despite the humiliation; what woman wouldn't? Though she had the satisfaction of knowing that the mistress's evening was spoilt too. Her face, Francine said, when they finally turned up, was the face of someone who knows she has been hideously used. A taste of usings to come – and yet she didn't drop him. Perhaps it's not Francine who is blind about Lionel, but Lionel who is capable of blinding anyone. Why do I say Francine is blind about Celia? Like father like daughter? I have no evidence. Nothing at all.

I leave early so I can call in at the bank on my way home and arrange sterling transfers to Poland; for once our contacts there have given us the correct tedious but essential banking details. Back at the flat I change into leggings, and then run out of town to see Nick.

I'm at the cottage in less than twenty minutes. I've hardly broken into a sweat. The front door is closed but unlocked, so I let myself in. It's a gloomy, grey evening but the lights aren't on. The living room is empty. Somehow, though, I know Nick is here. I sense a human presence.

I walk through to the conservatory out the back.

It's a glassed-in veranda, really. A long thin room where in sunshine you need dark glasses and at night you can see the stars. When the weather's bad you can watch the wind wuthering, the rain beating. It makes you feel part of things.

Nick is here. Sitting silently in the gloom. Something is wrong. He looks so still, so oddly immobile that I immediately wonder if he's been drinking. Spirit drinking. Too much beer makes him loud and impossible, wine turns him gooey, but spirits cut him off, put a stranger behind his eyes. The only time I've ever been frightened of Nick – though I needn't have been, as it turned out – was an occasion he was drunk on spirits. But he is not, normally, a drinker. Alcohol plays havoc with your coordination.

And I can't smell anything. I squat on my heels in front of the chair and say, 'You all right?'

'I'm not sure,' he says, very quietly.

My brain cells scatter. He sounds frightened. I remain silent for a moment to compose myself. There's definitely no smell of alcohol.

Then I see that there is a book in his lap. I stand up and turn on the light. Nick blinks as if the brightness hurts; he's been in the gloom a while.

I pick up the book. It's a hardback entitled *Macrobiotic Miracle: How a Vermont Family Overcame Cancer.* I turn it over. There is a photo of a white middle-aged woman on the back, smiling to camera. The text says, *The startling true story of Vanessa White, diagnosed as having malignant melanoma, fourth stage, who cured herself with a macrobiotic diet.* Across the text, in red diagonal letters are the words, *There is a choice.*

Fourth stage. Nobody's said anything to us about stages.

I put the book down on the table beside Nick.

'Pete sent it,' he says. Pete is a lawyer in Vancouver. He cares about Nick. They were friends in their teens. Nick's sister must have told him.

'You don't need it,' I say. 'You're cured.' I am angry with Pete. Books like this suggest you could help yourself. Maybe you could, but we don't want to hear it now. The corollary is that you have damaged yourself. That you have done something wrong, eaten unhealthy foods, lived the wrong life. That it's all your fault. It is not helpful. Anyway, Nick is cured. He doesn't need help.

'I've got spots on the scar.' Nick's voice is paper thin. Report anything unusual, the doctors told him before he left hospital. Anything at all. And keep an eye on the cancer site. If my mind is blanking, what is happening to his?

'Let me see.' I must not panic. These are the moments that I have to be strong. He's looked at the book, scared himself, and then looked at his leg. Poor Nick.

He stands up and undoes his belt. I don't have to persuade him. My eyes are what he wants. A second opinion. He is braver than I am. If I had cancer, I would never check myself. I never check my breasts now. I am much too scared of finding anything. But Nick had been told to inspect himself, so he does. He has never asked me to do it. He does it himself, though every inspection must terrify.

I sit on the edge of the chair he's vacated and turn his thigh to the light. The flesh under my fingers still feels wooden, abnormally hard. But the scar, the site of the original cancer, is well healed now. It's a long thin line, like a sword cut. Neat and still pink, but with that oyster sheen to it that tells you it will soon be white. It's nearly an old scar.

'Where?' I can't see anything sinister.

'Three spots.' Nick starts to show me, but I've seen them already. They are tiny. I peer at them closely. Pink pimples, smaller even than the hair-follicle pimples you get on the back of your arms.

'They're stitch scars, aren't they? Surely? They're in a line.'

'I've never noticed them before.'

He checks himself every day. I have to believe him. But at the same time, these are so regular, so evenly spaced. They look man-made.

I turn my wrist. It's five forty-five.

'You go to the surgery,' I say. 'Now.'

The local doctors weren't involved in the treatment of his melanoma, except for the original referral, and a couple of them might not even understand what has been done. But they'll all have seen a melanoma at some stage, on someone, and they'll all have seen young scars. Nick needs the voice of authority.

He doesn't argue. He understands better than I how not knowing is worse than knowing even the worst. He is a sensible person. He does as he knows he should.

He rings the surgery and the receptionist says a doctor will see him straight away. Everyone at the health centre takes him seriously. It's both reassuring and scary. He throws on his coat, picks up his car keys, and leaves.

Left on my own, it's headless chicken time. If I went out for another run now I might never come back. I can't sit down. Much as I disapprove of doing Nick's housework for him now he's stronger, I find myself emptying the overflowing bin in the kitchen, and clearing magazines from the tiled veranda floor. I pick up dozens of custom-car magazines – magazines that he still buys, despite having done nothing creative to his thirty-year-old car since he started working evenings at the Playhouse two years ago. While I'm stacking the magazines I suddenly stop. I wonder why I haven't gone to the surgery with Nick. Why I'm making the agony longer for myself than it needs to be. Why, when he's so frightened, I'm not at his side. I tell myself that my presence, my insistence on accompanying him, when he didn't ask me to, would have frightened him more. This way the panic is his alone. Staying here is an act of reassurance, of refusal to be panicked. That is the reason. Nothing to do with cowardice.

I keep noticing the Canadian book on the table. I'd like to throw it in the black plastic rubbish bag but superstition kicks in and I can't do it. If I throw it away, because of course Nick's cured, he might turn out not to be. Fate won't be second guessed.

I remember that I read something else about cancer this week. Or rather, noticed the article, before skipping deliberately over it. It was about personality types, and stress – almost the tactless, self-inflicted injury line. It does seem to be true, though, that vulnerable people get cancer. The bereaved, the depressed, the desperately unhappy. But you can't help being bereaved, depressed or unhappy, can you? Or is the crux how you cope with these things? I once read that breast cancer in women was related to suppressed aggression. Though I didn't believe it, even then.

Anyway, Nick is not, now, especially vulnerable. He is not, in his ordinary day-to-day life, under abnormal stress. He has gone to considerable trouble, living out here, away from the pressure of city life, to ensure he is not stressed. If he had developed a serious illness eleven years ago, when he was trying to rejoin the group after his accident, it would perhaps have been more understandable. Because his return didn't work. The doctors declared him physically recovered, but psychologically something had changed. Maybe it's as he says: when his body was shocked, his eyes were opened. What he had been prepared to put up with in the past – the overloaded, frenetic schedules, the exhausting, mind-fogging travel, the hustle, the claustrophobic living, the promotional crap – he could take no longer. No one, he says, should be expected to. He suffered acute disorientation and anxiety symptoms – manifested in an almost total inability to concentrate – and shed a stone in weight. His co-players grew impatient with his distractedness and alarmed at his emaciation and, with the agreement of the group's management, finally issued an ultimatum: get whatever professional help he needed – and they'd organize or pay for the best – or get out. He chose out. He still finds multiple stimuli difficult. Crowds of strangers in unfamiliar, noisy places. That's why he doesn't like parties; or thinks he doesn't. He still doesn't travel, if he can help it. He is, in a mild way, travel phobic.

But he's dealt with that. He's reorganized his life so that it suits him, and isn't stressful. After the initial push, nobody had to take him in hand and organize him. He looked at what he disliked, or couldn't do any longer, and made sensible, adult decisions about them. He moved here. He slowly, unfrenetically, built himself a new career. He recognizes his limitations. He prefers the familiar to the unknown, so he sticks to the known. He rarely travels, even now, but if he has to – like when his mother died, for example, and he needed to be with his father – he drives (usually in a hired car) because that puts him in control, but avoids all motorways, because they take the control away again. On A and B roads he can escape, or stop, if he wants to. He knows that his foibles label him neurotic, but he has never felt impelled to do anything about them, partly because at a deep, recalcitrant level, he believes his feelings are rational, and partly because, living here, he doesn't need to. Here, he is a normal, competent, coping person. And yet, he has cancer.

I make myself sit down in the living room and try to read his *Independent.* On the very front page the word *cancer* leaps out at me. Christ. I snatch my eyes away. Not before I've seen that it's about a cancer charity, and a fall in donations. It seems, sometimes, that cancer's everywhere you look. Like being pregnant, Francine says. Suddenly the whole world is pregnant, or has advice for those who are. I wouldn't know; but it's certainly true about cancer. I cannot read a paper or magazine at the moment without falling over the word. During the summer everyone wanted to warn you about skin cancer. I almost gave up reading. I know nothing more about it now than I did before Nick was ill, except what I have seen him directly experience. No doctor has enlightened us. We can't blame them; we could have been persistent, and demanded their attention, their explanations, but we didn't. They didn't offer information – or the offers they made fell through – and we didn't push for it. We were too frightened.

And now tiny red dots on Nick's scar are terrifying us. Because we don't know what we should be looking for, or what we should be scared of. We're like children, frightened of shadows, frightened of anything.

I spot Toby the cat, snoozing on a pile of lintner's felt on Nick's sewing machine table. Lintner's felt is what is used to line upholstery leather with to give it that luxurious padded feel. The sewing machine used to be mine and has been sitting here, unused, along with the felt remnants, for at least a couple of years. Since Nick finished upholstering the interior of his car.

I pick Toby up and cuddle him. His limbs feel very old and stiff these days. But his tummy is round and full. Perhaps a bit too round. Maybe he's got worms.

'Purr for me, Toby,' I whisper. I hold him over my shoulder as I pace the room. Up to the guitar cases and stands, the amps and bundles of leads, the music end. Back down to the sofa and television and Muriel, out of her case as usual. And, sweet cat, he does start purring. Right in my ear. It makes my eyes water.

And then I hear Nick's car outside. The engine stop. The thunk of the driver's door. A silence, as he walks up the drive. I put the cat down. The front door rattles.

He says, 'Stitch scars. You were right,' before he's properly inside the room. He understands the terror of the moment. My body hears him, and unfreezes.

He walks straight up to me and grips me, hard, by the shoulders. It is almost, but not quite, an embrace. We stand still. Then I move closer, to show that I don't blame him for the terror.

I feel his body relax. 'Sorry, sorry, Jess,' he whispers.

And I murmur, 'Oh God, oh God,' which is half thanksgiving for now, half fervent prayer for the future.

Chapter 3

Two days after Nick came home from hospital, that first time, he hobbled down to lunch on his huge tight tender giant's leg, and during the meal I was provoked to say, 'D'you have to groan so much? It's very off-putting,' and he said, 'Sorry. But it helps. I like doing it.'

He looked well. Relatively speaking. Well for someone nine days after a six-hour operation. Kind of pinkly, bright-eyed well. Deceptively well, as it turned out. I should have touched him.

He sat in the living room all afternoon, doing nothing. Didn't even take Muriel out of her case. By tea-time the brightness in his eyes had become a glitter and around seven, just before supper, he had to haul himself back to bed. His leg, he said, felt like lead.

I took his temperature. I knew he was feverish by now – the heat was radiating off him – but I needed figures. I rang his GP, Dr Francis, and asked if he would expect someone to be running a temperature of 101 degrees nine days after a major operation. He said no, he certainly wouldn't, and that he was coming over. I didn't have to ask.

He arrived in less than thirty minutes. I led him upstairs and he took Nick's temperature again. Nick asked what it was, and he said it was, 'Going a bit.' He looked in Nick's mouth and his ears, and listened to his chest. Just in the half hour since I'd made the phone call Nick seemed more prostrated, more ill. I stood in the doorway of the bedroom and watched the two men. Dr Francis is my doctor too, or rather, one of mine – it's a large practice – but I'd never seen him and Nick together before. I was struck by how similar they were: both early thirties, both dark, straight-haired, tallish. One standing, one lying down. One ill, one well. I didn't like seeing Dr Francis as an ordinary human being. As a real, possibly fallible, young man.

He asked for the names of Nick's doctors at the hospital, and said he needed to phone. I took him downstairs. He rang the hospital and started chasing members of the surgeon's team, while I went off to make him a cup of tea. When I returned he was speaking to someone, so I left the mug beside him and went back upstairs.

After a few minutes he rejoined us and said he'd failed to track down the consultant, but had spoken to the Senior Registrar. He looked unhappy and said, 'He's left the decision to me.' One doctor won't criticize another, but I felt he was close to it. He shook his head and said, 'Well, I'm out of my depth. So he goes back. OK?'

I moaned, 'Oh God,' but Nick didn't say anything. He wasn't up to any response by then. Dr Francis went back downstairs to call an ambulance, and thank God he did. Thank God he came quickly when we called him, and moved fast when he got here.

The ambulance arrived soon after nine and two gentle ambulance men took Nick away. There was no question of my accompanying him; I was given a number to ring first thing in the morning to find out where and how he was. Ambulances seem much larger, close to, than they look wailing past you on the roads. When the vehicle disappeared it seemed to leave a hole in the dusk. I went back into the cottage and the quietness hissed at me. I wondered if I should ring Paul; whether it was my duty to terrify him too, a near-seventy-year-old father, helpless two hundred miles away. I decided it wasn't. I told myself I'd leave phoning him till the next day, after I'd made my own call, when I would know more and, maybe, could sound more reassuring. I watched a film on the television about young men on motorbikes chasing each other across Australia, and at midnight started to watch another, a Spanish comedy with subtitles. I knew that if I made a decision to go home or upstairs to sleep I wouldn't, so I fell asleep on the sofa, with Toby on my stomach and the television still chattering.

Nick went back to the same ward but, this time, instead of being in a four-bed room, he was put next to the nurses' station in a single room, where he could lie naked on top of the sheet with the interior blinds drawn and a bedside electric fan cooling him. The infection was in the abdominal wound, not the leg. The doctors had taken swabs and the first antibiotics they'd pumped into him proved to be the right ones; even so, the bug was deeply resistant. It was several days before Nick surfaced into full consciousness, and even then he couldn't eat, and only wanted to drink ginger beer.

The evening of the first day I rang Paul and simply told him what had happened; that this was nothing to do with the cancer, just a post-op complication that could happen to anyone. That Nick honestly wasn't up to visitors, just at present, but that I'd ring every day, and he mustn't worry.

Two weeks passed in a blur of anxiety, of squeaky-tiled hospital corridors, the white noise of air-conditioning, shadowless artificial light, increasingly familiar, tedious car journeys, Demeter work when I could, and midnight running. At the end of the fortnight Nick was still feverish, and clear liquid started to seep from the stitch line in his side. If he moved it became a watery gush.

The first time this happened was at night, when he couldn't see the colour of the liquid, and he thought he was haemorrhaging. The nurses rushed in when he shouted, switched the lights on and calmed him, and put plastic sheets on the bed. The doctors called the infection an abscess, and said they'd have to re-open the wound. It would mean another anaesthetic. Nick, for a half day after they told him, lay still on the bed, eyes closed, flattened with despair.

But in fact the operation was short and minor – because all they did was open the wound, pack it with wadding, and leave it open – and he was back on the ward in an hour. I waited in his room for him. He had had no pre-operative sedation and was conscious when he returned, but the anaesthetic drugs made him emotional; at least, it was the drugs he blamed – he couldn't stop tears streaming from the corners of his eyes. He was very low. We both were. I remember driving home that night and thinking: thank God we don't have children. Imagine him being this ill, and me this frightened and exhausted, with children. And then I thought: but if we had children, I'd be a different person. A wiser person. Not such a kid myself. I'd be more in touch with the rhythms of life, with birth, death, the whole thing. And then I thought: why the hell should motherhood do that to you? Of course this would be just as terrible; no less bearable. It would – I was right first time – be worse. You just think that mothers can cope. That's what they do, cope. And then

I thought of my own mother, and amended that to some mothers. Normal mothers.

And then I imagined Nick dying without ever having children and a coldness crept into me, stiffening my bones. When I got home I couldn't run or eat or anything. It was only nine o'clock, and the middle of July, but I had to go to bed immediately with a hot-water bottle.

That was rock bottom. Around that time I found it hard to ring anyone, because of being forced to listen to the cracks in my own voice. My mother started inviting me to visit. She left messages that said, *Jess, you are doing too much. You are never in when I ring. The hospital is miles away. Nick can't expect you to visit every day.* She didn't understand that my visits had nothing to do with Nick's expectations. She knew he was ill, but didn't understand how ill, because I didn't tell her. I couldn't face her knowing; her sympathy, I thought, would break me. And I continued to protect Paul. Not from the facts – he had a father's right to know – but from my fear. I told him it would be better if he visited when Nick's fever had gone. I assured him Nick was in safe, competent hands. He was in no real danger. I reassured, and soothed. I rang Jason, because he needed to know what was going on, but no one else. No one else rang me, or, if they did – and my mother was right, I was rarely in – they didn't leave messages. Jason told me that several people rang him, but not people who'd tried me first: people who didn't like to 'bother' me. I saw Francine, after she returned from holiday the third week in July, but no one else. There was no time to see people. And soon it was too late anyway, because there was too much to tell. It was easier to stay out of touch.

But then Nick began to improve. The draining operation was a success. His side stopped gushing. His temperature was still volatile, but lower than it had been. His swollen leg began to look horrible, but this was apparently expected, by everyone except us. This was what the chemical profusion did to legs. The flesh turned yellow and the skin peeled off. His toe-nails were loosening. The ball of his foot had developed a hard separating crust and when it finally split, Nick said, the foot butterfly was going to emerge. He was definitely feeling better. Sister tried to pick at the crust, sneakily, whenever she stood at the bottom of his bed, as she had a habit of doing when she came in to gossip about the doctors. She'd take a surreptitious pick, and Nick would bawl at her. She told him he was quite right, and not to take crap from anyone.

Then he asked for Muriel. The day I took her in, and watched him tune her up and fuss over what the hospital air-conditioning might do to her, but decide to keep her with him anyway, was the day I knew he would, eventually, be coming home. He started to joke with Sister about the pain-killing shots she gave him when she changed the wadding in his open wound. (The flesh was still sensitive then, the nerve endings hadn't yet given up.) He told her to shoot the painkiller all over his abdomen and thigh, so he could bear Muriel's weight across his body more comfortably. She told him she'd jab his fingers if he didn't hold still and shut up. She started to call him Mr Guitar Man, and said it wasn't his hands that needed exercise now but the rest of him, and he should stop playing so much and get off his backside. He tried, but couldn't manage even the short walk to his armchair because his foot had become so tender. So she issued him with a sheepskin-lined bootee, and then a stick, to make it even easier. Suddenly he could walk again.

He took over responsibility for keeping his father informed. He rang him on the portable hospital phone and persuaded him not to visit. He promised to ring every couple of days instead. Paul didn't argue, as he might have done if I'd tried to put him off; the sound of Nick's voice must have been more reassuring and convincing than any words from me, and probably more reassuring and convincing than actually seeing him. This last point, I think, was in Nick's mind too, and the reason he didn't want his father to visit. He had seen himself in mirrors by now, the pallor and thinness of his face, the wreck of his leg, and didn't want to frighten Paul.

I asked if I could take Nick home. He was obviously improving, he needed to come home. I started to grow anxious that the recovery wouldn't last, that the hospital which had given him one infection would give him another. He had to be safer in his own home, with his own dirt and cat hairs, his own germs. Sister was sympathetic. So, I was told, were the doctors. Sister made him his latex bung, and taught him how to look after it. She encouraged him to take long slow strolls, wearing his bootee and leaning heavily on his stick, round the hospital. One day he got up to the roof. On another he went down to the main ground-floor concourse. When he got to the automatic glass entrance doors a security guard emerged from a cubby hole and asked if everything was all right. Nick pointed his stick at the cars outside and said he was thinking of nicking one and driving home. The guard said, 'Right you are, sir,' and returned to his cubicle. Nick said the encounter was amusing but also, because of what it said about his apparent capabilities, deeply depressing.

He was finally discharged the first week of August, five weeks after the original operation. On the day of his discharge Sister put his 4.00 p.m. fever down to the cup of tea he'd just had, and said, 'Get out before I change my mind.' With our carrier bags of bandages and antiseptics and elastic stockings we fled. As fast as Nick's leg would allow.

His recovery held. Apart from weekly visits to the bung clinic he didn't have to go back. His temperature only fluttered up once or twice, and never to alarming levels. He started to eat, and he stopped losing weight. He looked truly convalescent, at last.

The funny thing was that Nick being so ill for those weeks distracted us, both of us: he was so unwell, so incapable of seeing beyond the short term, and I was so frightened, so tired, and so anxious, and then, later, so relieved. We forgot, for a short while, about the cancer.

Nick has agreed to give Celia guitar lessons. She's had four already. He teaches her at the shop, like anyone else, in the curtained-off back room. This rear space is his storeroom-cum-workshop, with bench and vices, racks of files and pliers and sandpaper and glue and all the other paraphernalia of string-instrument maintenance and minor repair. It's not really separate from the shop but he teaches there as a matter of principle: learners, he says, should get used to the idea of being overheard from the first, however excruciating the noise they are making. That way they won't become closet musicians, who can play perfectly to an empty room, or the family pet, but freeze in front of a human audience. As he points out, making music is essentially a group activity. Of course, being so close to the front shop does also mean he's available if Jason needs him, which is convenient for the business, too.

I still hate the idea of the lessons but as I can formulate no rational reason for this I haven't made my opposition public. I have even tried to ridicule myself out of it, by telling myself that I have a soap-opera view of the Brackenbury family. Lionel the megalomaniac arch-seducer. Francine the selfless saint. Celia the manipulative bitch-child, young Philip – what? – his mother's avenger? (I rather like the boy; or feel sorry for him, anyway.)

But the real reason, I think, is that I am feeling generally depressed and self-pitying. It's been creeping up on me for weeks. As Nick recovers – and he's fitter and stronger every day – I seem to be going downhill. The last twenty-four hours have been particularly black and miserable. I lay in bed last night alone in my flat and wallowed: just let the self-pity run. Why not, in the privacy of your own head-space? I thought: no one will ever know what I suffered this last summer. What Nick and I suffered. I've protected Nick's father from it. And my mother. I have never told anyone the truth. Almost as if by denying my distress to others, I've been trying to protect myself. But if so, it's a mistake. It doesn't work. You frighten yourself much more, carrying fear alone, than others would reflect back to you, if you shared it. And I have been assuming, stupidly, that eventually the truth will out. People will learn of our ordeal, somehow, even if I don't tell them. But this isn't going to happen. Time is passing, people's lives and thoughts move on, and we – I – will never have justice. The Sister at the hospital said something that stuck in my mind: the doctors treat the wound, the nurses treat the patient, no one treats the relatives. I count myself, in Nick's case, a relative.

Is this battle fatigue? Am I depressed now simply from exhaustion? And am I exhausted now because, for the first time, it's safe to be exhausted? Because, at last,

I can afford to let my guard down? Is it safe to think that?

See, fear still controls my thoughts.

Today, outside, it is a bitter late-November Saturday morning. I was at the town library earlier, returning a couple of unread, overdue books, but now I'm sheltering in Nick's shop, keeping Jason company while Nick finishes a lesson with Celia behind the rear curtain. I'm not quite sure why I'm here, although Nick and I do occasionally have Saturday lunch together. The front room of the shop isn't large, and the wood-trellised walls are almost completely hidden behind hanging instruments and shelves of accessories, sheet music and primer books. The guitars, acoustic and electric, occupy most space; there's no room for large instruments like pianos though there are a couple of electronic keyboards. Nick supplies classical string instruments for sale or school hire but keeps only one – his own old cello – in the shop. The front display area contains a glossy selection of brass instruments and saxophones – partly because they look attractive, and partly because the local comprehensive school headmaster complains that too few pupils take up brass instruments these days and wants Nick to push them. Two customers, a teenaged boy and his father – who just admitted to Jason that he played guitar himself when he was young, and will clearly fight his son for possession of any instrument they buy – have just left, clutching catalogues and price lists.

I'm cold and low-spirited, wrapped up in a thick padded jacket over a fleecy tracksuit. I know I look horrible; I've seen myself in a couple of shop windows and the slimline, energetic, ready-for-anything me has disappeared. I look like something someone has deliberately overinflated to have a good laugh at.

'How's she doing?' I ask Jason. Quietly, since there's no one else in the shop. We can hear the odd twang. And Nick's voice, though I can't pick out any words.

Jason, being an innocent, has no idea that what I'm looking for is a contemptuous sneer, or a lofty, 'She tries . . .' Instead he looks enthused and says, 'Ah, coming along great, honest.'

Sweet boy. Sweet, stupid, infuriating boy. He has no ego at all. No agenda of his own, which is why he doesn't understand those of others. What purpose in life he does have seems entirely subsumed into the promotion and exaltation of others. Nick, specifically, but me too, by association. We are, in every aspect, it would seem, entirely admirable. We can do no wrong. Jason is the easiest person in the world to get along with – his thoughts, his feelings, are spread before you like a generous, ardently devoted rug. At least, the Jason we see. He has parents, several sisters, a town full of friends. Perhaps to them he is a selfish, cynical, uncooperative youth, but I doubt it. How did he acquire such an attractive, willing, guileless personality?

One can only assume that some individuals are so internally secure that they can wear their character openly, whatever its faults, without any sense of being diminished or made vulnerable by such exposure. As if they have cracked, intuitively, the essential truth that to admit to imperfections goes a long way to negating them. Jason is also little and dark and pretty, and smiles nearly all the time, bless him.

I rub my nose, which has no feeling in it, and discover it is slightly damp. I sniff, while trying to find a handkerchief in my coat pocket.

'Be finished any minute now,' says Jason. He assumes I'm waiting for Nick. Ah, I've found a grubby tissue. Am I waiting for Nick?

'How's the trumpet playing going?' I blow my nose. In a better mood I might have found the association of trumpet playing and nose blowing amusing. In my present mood I merely note this.

Jason nods enthusiastically. 'Gettin' there.' Nick is paying for Jason to learn the trumpet. He feels that one or other of them should be able to play every instrument they stock, or hire, if only to demonstration level. Nick covers the string instruments, obviously, and woodwind and reed – including saxophone – to a lower but still competent level, while Jason plays drums and harmonica well enough to perform on both (not simultaneously) in local bands. Both he and Nick can produce something on keyboards, though Jason can't read piano music. But brass instruments have gone undemonstrated. Nick feels this is a serious omission, especially given his chat with the school headmaster, so he has borrowed a trumpet from a fellow dealer and pays for Jason to have lessons in working hours from a local Salvation Army trumpeter.

The curtain across the entrance to the back room is pulled aside and Celia emerges. She is, I have to admit, a quite lovely girl. I want to cry. Nick is behind her and he doesn't see me immediately, so I have a chance to study him as he exists without me, in the company of a beautiful nineteen-year-old.

Well, he's not immune. Self-pity is pushing me, but I can't honestly say more than that. He looks attentive and engaged, but hardly drooling. Jason's expression is actually more irritating. It is as friendly and puppyish as when he greets me.

Celia's colour is high, which doesn't suit everyone, but flatters her. Her white-blond hair falls in a silky bob to her chin and she is dressed in soft figurehugging leather trousers, a crisp white linen shirt, and tailored waistcoat. Her outdoor coat, which Jason hands her after relieving her of her pretty, mother-of-pearl-inlaid guitar, is not a Michelin Man duvet anorak but a long midnight-blue woollen cloak-like garment which hangs perfectly and which will swing from her shoulders as she walks. She hasn't yet recognized me.

Nick has though, and cries, 'Hi, Jess!' I hear his welcome as slightly overdone. I imagine him relieved not to have been caught being overfamiliar with Celia.

Celia's eyes open wider, and she smiles at me.

'Jason tells me you're coming along well,' I say. I think I'm returning her smile.

Celia turns and says, 'Am I, Nick?'

The use of his first name is presumptuous. Excessively so. I hate her. Her expression is coy. Little bitch.

Nick replies briskly, 'Course you are.'

'Sounds good to me,' Jason says. Celia catches his eye and drops her gaze. Jason grins. Not having a shy corpuscle in his body, he finds the blushes of others hilarious. Actually I'm not sure that Celia is shy, in this instance; she may just be trying to discourage him.

'Till Thursday, then,' she says to Nick, and Nick says, 'Right.'

'See you,' I say. Which I probably will, at the Brackenbury house, on several occasions during the working week.

Celia's lips frame the words, 'Bye,' as she passes me, though no sound is audible. I don't think her eyes focus on me.

Once she's gone Nick grabs his coat, which, I realize, is remarkably like hers. Long and dark and much too good for escorting someone impersonating an ill-used beach ball. He says, 'Be back at two, Jason,' then tips his head at the door and says, 'Come with me, Jess.'

Have I been rude? Is he going to tell me off? I smile brightly at Jason, give him a farewell wave, and follow Nick out of the shop. Outside, he takes my elbow and hustles me up the road, and then into the alleyway that leads to the rear yard where he parks his car. Half-way down he pulls me to a halt.

'Yes?' I say.

'What's wrong?'

'What makes you think anything's wrong?'

He rolls his eyes. He has known me a long time.

'I'm depressed,' I say. 'I don't know why. Maybe it's Christmas.'

'It's weeks till Christmas.'

'I'm not happy.' My eyes fill with tears. I'm pathetic. Grace just met me in Safeways and asked how I was and I said: fine, fine. To Grace. Why do I do it?

Nick puts his arms around me. It's not really human contact because his coat and the cushioning of my jacket are between us, but it's enough to make my throat ache.

'There's no reason for it,' I mumble. 'That's what's so stupid.'

Nick rocks me from side to side. What can he say? *I know I'm the reason, but I can't help having cancer?* How can I burden him with this when he, truly, is the vulnerable one?

Then something pops into my mind. It's got nothing to do with this, but it suddenly seems so vital that I pull back to say it.

'Toby's ill.' He was on my lap last night and I was stroking him. His side was hard and swollen. I've only just acknowledged what I felt.

There's a short silence. Then Nick says, 'I know.' Another silence, as if he's debating how much to tell me. 'The vet says he's not in any pain. He's probably got a couple of months. Just to leave him alone.'

'Oh shit.' How grotesque. How can fate be so cruel? I have to look away from Nick; eyes are so treacherous – I can't risk what might pass, involuntarily, between us. How long has he known, and why didn't he tell me before? I start to cry. Though everything's a muddle; I'm not sure what horror I'm crying at.

'Hey.' Nick pulls me on down the alleyway to the back yard, and his car. He unlocks it. This vehicle is a joke. A left-over joke. He can only get away with it because he so rarely drives anywhere. He took up car restoration a decade ago when he thought his career had reached a dead end, and wanted a hobby that wasn't music. But then slowly lost interest – or the time to pursue the interest, anyway – as music commitments rebuilt. It was always an odd hobby for him; even he could see the paradox in playing with objects whose main purpose – travel – he disliked so much. But he is attracted to the visual and iconic, not the utilitarian side of cars. Anyway, he gave up sensible restoration after his old Jag was stolen. This vehicle was originally one of the old finned Mark III Zephyr-Zodiacs and had been mechanically rebuilt before he acquired it. Someone else's half-completed project, which suited Nick because he's much more proficient at body work and trim and general car aesthetics than at mechanics. The car is long and low and sharklike and worth nothing in any purist's book. The exterior is black and looks vaguely dangerous. Nick believes all cars should look dangerous, because that's what they are. The rounded, cute, safe-looking, Fisher-Price school of styling is, in his view, criminally dishonest. The Zodiac looks tatty these days but is nevertheless enjoyable to be a passenger in, because of its generous dimensions, its beautiful and comfortable handmade leather upholstery, and, despite its decrepitudes, its undeniable pose appeal.

Nick doesn't tell me not to cry on the red leather. 'Maybe I'm sickening for something,' I sniff, as we pull out of the yard. We accelerate up the High Street. A foot in front of me, above the in-car CD player, a horizontal red line zooms across the dash. This is the speedo. Designed on a preposterous scale, to make any motion feel fast; we're actually only doing thirty-one miles an hour.

'Dad rang this morning,' Nick says. 'He's definitely coming for Christmas.'

I nod. Make the effort to stop thinking about myself. If Nick can cope – with so much more to cope with – why can't I? It's going to be happy families at Christmas. Nick and Paul, me and my mum. She asked, and I couldn't say no. I haven't seen her face to face since Nick was ill. I never took her up on her escape offers, so it's been months and months. And Nick's still alive. I can crow now, can't I?

In a few minutes we're outside Nick's cottage. 'I'll

make you lunch,' he says, as we get out. 'And you can take that stupid coat off.'

He has noticed how ugly I am. I feel my mouth pull into a wail, but I manage to suppress any noise. I follow him to the cottage. Inside I pick Toby up. The lump is hard, the hardest thing on his body. Poor, poor cat. I squeeze him so tightly he struggles to escape.

I take off my stupid coat and go up to the bathroom. And there discover red wine stains on the tissue. I'm bleeding, days early. I feel ridiculous relief; it's my body cracking up, not me. I am not really depressed, I don't have to look for reasons, it's all hormones.

I leave the bathroom and track Nick down to the kitchen. From the doorway I say, 'I've just started my period.'

He's warming up soup on the stove, his back to me, still wearing his long, graceful black coat. He's heard me; he nods twice, over the saucepan. But he says nothing. He has learned not to say, 'What a surprise,' or 'Fancy that,' when I'm frail-tempered and present him with this news.

But today, because I want to believe in a female cause myself, I wish he wasn't so tactful.

Chapter 4

Having cancer does not make you a better person. Having *had* cancer, and definitely survived, possibly might. You do occasionally read about people who, regarding themselves as exceptionally lucky, or as having cheated fate in some way, become – presumably in a rush of thankfulness – almost evangelically altruistic. They form self-help groups for others; raise huge sums for cancer charities, or for the hospitals that saved them. They extend helping hands to others further back on the cancer road. And the experience of having had cancer might well make them better-balanced, clearer-sighted, wiser individuals. Good for them. There's a cancer self-help group here in town; I've seen their poster in the surgery. The number is 831189. Nick must have seen it too. You notice the word *cancer* when your life is affected by it. But we've never rung the number. We've never even mentioned it.

Having had cancer and not survived, of course, makes you a much worse person. Well, to put it bluntly, an irretrievably dead person. And, on the way there, a shocked, befuddled, anxious, unhappy, frightened, desperate, raging, exhausted and finally defeated person. The late, dead, defeated Nicholas Baker.

Shut up, Jess. Nick is neither of these. Neither a person with cancer, nor a survivor of cancer. He is a person who has had cancer, and who may or may not still have it, lurking somewhere silently within him, and who doesn't yet know if he is going to survive. The state of not knowing is a state impossible to come to terms with. Fear and hope, partners in crime. Nick is not a better person than he was before he had cancer; he is the same Nick he has always been, only under tremendous mental strain, and, still, not as physically strong as he was. Both cause him to be more easily tired, more easily irritated, and generally tenser than he was before.

You imagine that traumas such as cancer draw you together. It's true that some superficial nonsense falls away. I don't care any longer how messily Nick eats his boiled eggs – I'm just glad he's here to bash their heads in. It is immaterial to me, these days, whether he puts his shirt on first, when getting dressed, or his underpants. But at a more important level we are not drawn closer together. Rather the reverse: we are revealed, under a stark, merciless light, as separate people. My fate, possibly, is being unentwined from his. Or maybe it isn't. That's the problem. We don't know.

Do we talk about it? Do we draw closer that way? Do we shrink the fear demons to shadows by exposing them, exploring them, sharing them? Do we hell. We don't explore anything. We don't want to. Or, I assume we don't. We haven't even explored whether we want to explore anything.

We can talk about the cancer. We use the word; it's not taboo. Not at all. Nick tells everyone who wants or needs to know that he's had cancer. Neither of us find it difficult. We can cope with the past. What we avoid, verbally, is the future. Sentences that begin *if it came back* or *if I died* or *assuming I survive* or even *next year*. We avoid externalizing the future. Making the fear flare.

Of course we should speak about it. Or, at least, I assume we should. Nobody actually gives you a handbook. Though I bet one exists – the self-help groups probably stock them. But anyway, we can't do it. You handle things the best you can. In these circumstances you're not dealing with sensible, obedient, rationally minded others. You're dealing with yourself.

We do, outwardly, the same things now that we did before Nick had cancer. We follow the same routines. Nick is putting in his usual four and a half days at the shop – leaving Jason in sole charge on Mondays, the quietest day – and two evenings at the Playhouse. I work, as always, eight-thirty to five-ish at Demeter

Monday to Friday, and see Nick every other evening, at minimum, and half as many mornings. While we are following our routines we look normal. But it's an illusion; nothing is back to normal. It won't be, it can't be, for months, even if nothing untoward occurs. Maybe years. Nick has five years, at least, of check-ups in front of him. For the first year they're every three months. He's had one already. They give him X-rays, blood tests. They are looking – actively looking – for recurrence. How can we be normal? We're not making love like we used to. I'm very aware of this. We're still much too gentle, much too considerate of each other. Neither of us can take the brakes off. I'm scared of hurting him. He's scared of . . . I don't know. We haven't discussed it. Letting go? Letting what go? Would it be better if he wasn't so brave? So good at holding himself together?

It's two days before Christmas, which Nick and I will be celebrating with his father and my mother, and Nick is behaving like a typical, despicable man. That is, he's leaving everything to me. Even the thinking, which everyone knows is the hardest part. I remember, years ago, spending Christmas with Nick at his sister's, before she and her husband went to Canada. Nick and his brother-in-law slammed in from the pub at midnight and I remember the cry, no, howl, at a few minutes past, just after we had gone up to bed. Issuing from

Nick's sister, it transpired, after her husband had whispered in her ear, oh so innocently, *remind me, darling, what are we giving the children?*

I've been moaning about Nick to Francine in my office. There's hardly room for both of us in the room, after a van-load of petition-form boxes were delivered yesterday. Francine, in her usual passionate, impulsive, unthinking way, has agreed to take on the collection for an international tropical forests petition, which was being housed by an organization the other side of the country, but which has become very much more successful than anyone anticipated, and has exhausted their space. We've agreed to accommodate all the forms collected so far, as well as those to come. If we'd appreciated the physical aspects of the job I'm not sure we'd have been so keen. We have to keep all the petition forms here until next July, when they'll be delivered (by us, as our reward for storing them) to the Prime Minister at Downing Street. Some anniversary or other. Rio may have something to do with it. Don't ask me. I'm just the person with huge biceps who lugs boxes around.

My complaints about Nick have set Francine off. She's going to top my grievances with ones about Lionel. She's brimming with horror tales about him at the moment, because she's decided to divorce him. For the last half hour she's been clanging through the office filing cabinet, removing documents for her solicitor, but is now sitting on a three-stack of boxes at my side, her gaberdine-trousered legs (Francine would never wear jeans) neatly crossed. Her expression is almost beatific.

'Ten years ago, it must have been. Maybe eleven. Anyway. He brought eight friends back on Christmas Eve, without any warning at all, and insisted I entertain them, even though I was dropping after a day of cooking, last-minute shopping, and wrapping up presents. A complete nightmare. I got to bed at four, I think, and of course the children were up again at six. Then, after breakfast – so cruel – he gave the children their presents in the sitting room while I was still clearing away dishes and washing up. So I never saw their faces. I was terribly, terribly hurt. And then, on Christmas Day night, in front of two friends he'd also invited to the house without telling me, he gave me my Christmas present. It was a ruby ring. For all the hard work, he said, to show his appreciation. No doubt it cost a fortune. The friends thought he was wonderful. He probably sent his secretary out to get it. Or his mistress. I've never worn it. My pathetic revenge.'

Francine looks flushed, belligerently animated. She is gearing herself up for combat with Lionel, who is known to like a scrap. She's not a coward and can fight intellectual battles but is not a natural, I'd say, on a personal level. She'd be reluctant to go below the belt. Lionel is a terrific ally, but, by all accounts, a scary enemy, and wouldn't have any such qualms. Francine wants shares of the businesses she helped him set up. The ones where, even if he had most of the bright ideas, she did all the donkey work. The difficulty will be proving this. Only now is she grasping the significance of who signed what, where, and why. It is this depressing contractual evidence that she has just been extracting from the filing cabinet.

She slaps the folders on her lap and sighs. 'I'm not greedy, Jess. This is all for the sake of Demeter. I don't want to have to start paying myself a weekly wage.'

Talk of money reminds me. I've been meaning to have a word. 'Can I have a pay rise, Francine?' I say. 'I haven't had one for two years.'

'For two years?' Francine looks appalled.

'It's all right,' I say. 'I've managed.' But I'm not managing now. Or only just. In the last few months I've become alarmingly extravagant. Both Nick and I have. It's understandable in his case – why not have that Jackson-US guitar now, while he's alive to appreciate it? – but it seems to have rubbed off on me too. I bought myself a winter coat last week. Finally. A beautiful, grown-up, dry-clean-only, woollen coat. And a new pair of running shoes. Together they came to over two hundred pounds. I seem to have so many greater priorities than budgeting.

Francine puts her folders aside and takes down the accounts book to see how rich Demeter is. She gazes at the figures a while – accounts actually mean something to her – then snaps the book shut and says, 'OK. What about eight per cent? To cover both years. Backdate it to September. And next year, Jess, remind me.'

I nod obediently. It is my responsibility, Francine is saying, to keep track of my pay, and my fault, therefore, that a rise last year was overlooked. I understand about displaced defensiveness. Just for a while, Francine is going to be without fault. Unapologetically, uncompromisingly infallible. Fine by me.

After she's left the office I settle down to some routine correspondence and while my mind is free-roaming, realize that my earlier gripe about Nick is the first time I have criticized him to a third party since his cancer operation. I wonder if this is a good or a bad sign? I'm starting to let off steam. Part of me insists this is good – another step on the road to normality. The other knows it is risky. Suppose I can't take the criticism back? Suppose he drops down dead before I've retracted it? But he's not going to, is he, or not from cancer, anyway. Nothing happens instantly, with cancer. Plenty of time for retractions.

Even so, I feel an urgent need, superstitiously, to rush in with his good points. Yes, he can be infuriating. Diffident, exasperatingly unambitious. Nervy, off his own patch. In his youth he thought he was a rolling stone but he isn't; he needs his moss snug and secure around him. This makes him unadventurous. But he is a good friend. A good listener. He doesn't interrupt, unless I'm absolutely blabbering, and then only to calm me down, so he can listen better. Sometimes he hears me before I've said anything; he uses his eyes. When he's well, he lets me be physical with him, which I need. I can't stand to be hands off. Sometimes you can say things better with your body than with your mind. I know it's childish, and rather unfair, too, because usually I'm expressing aggressive feelings, and he doesn't have the same freedom, being a man and so much stronger. But I do need it. For when words would just come out, *plagh*. So, occasionally, we fight. Or we used to. It's one of the things I miss most at the moment.

And there's his talent, of course. I shouldn't really give credit to a quality that is God-given and I don't actually admire his musicianship as much as I used to; all mysteries lose their wonder eventually. But it gives him a quality, an extraordinary competency, which is separate from me and which I cannot, and could never, fathom, which I find deeply attractive. And although being musical is a gift, he has worked hard at developing and exploiting it. He still practices every day. He is as good a player – maybe better – as he ever was. He hasn't wasted the gift.

There; I've cancelled out the criticism, haven't I? Appeased the gods. I can move on now, with my conscience clear.

I leave work early to meet my mother off the five o'clock train. Driving to the station I feel jittery. When I last saw her, back in May, the world was a different, less problematic, much safer place. I feel I've changed. Will this alter anything between us?

But waiting on the platform of the small station – the staff are in the process of locking the ticket booth – I realize that nothing essential has changed. I experience the same feeling I always get when I'm about to see my mother. A feeling of tremendous, painful, longing. I yearn to see her – the train is coming in now, and I'm craning over the heads of other bystanders – yet know that when I do, she will, as usual, disappoint me.

There she is. Here she is. A plump, pink and white, velvet-complexioned woman, young-looking for sixty. I can see from her face that she needs something already.

'Mwoi, mwoi.' She kisses me, twice. Her kisses actually make a sound like that. She smells of peaches. 'The Ladies . . . darling . . . sorry, you know me . . .'

There must have been a lavatory on the train. Why didn't she use that? Luckily the station cloakrooms are still open. 'Over here,' I say, taking her case, and lead her towards them.

I wait outside. I am used to organizing things for my mother. My father left us when I was ten. My mother can't really be helpless – she has survived, more or less on her own, since I left home twelve years ago – but she is lazy about decision-making, and prefers not to make the effort. She is the antithesis of a control freak: completely content to let others lead, organize for her, pull her along in their wake. I was a tomboy before my father left; my mother swears that she never actually said, 'You're the man of the house now, dear,' but if she didn't, it must have been something close. I seemed to have the responsibility, almost the authority, all my teenage years. I feel my mother as a dependent weight.

She emerges from the Ladies. She has coped with her luggage all the way from Reading, including one change of trains, but suddenly it is all too much for her. She flutters and drops things. I take her magazines and umbrella and tow the suitcase behind me to the car.

'Mother,' I say, as she dithers near the boot, 'it's unlocked. Just get in.'

I know, as I stash the luggage, that my mother means well. I know that she loves me. Her trouble is that she thinks that appearing hopeless and dependent makes her attractive. That it endears her to you. It is a kind of compliment. It works, at least in the short term, with men. She's had a number of boyfriends. But it presumably didn't work in the long term with my father, and it exhausts me. It's not fair, I sometimes think. Other people have mothers with big arms and all the answers; I've got one who throws herself on me.

I drive her back to my flat. We're eating out later with Nick and his father, who arrived yesterday. My mother needs to shower and change. I usually take a run early evening – ending up at Nick's cottage, often – but forgo it tonight. I even think I'll dress up a bit. I spend a while deciding what to wear, and then have to decide what Mother is going to wear, too. The blue, I tell her, after she's waved alternatives at me; it's the outfit with fewest bows and buttons and fussy bits.

'And how is Paul?' Mother asks, as she finally approves herself in the mirror. She does wear her clothes well. Plumpness definitely flatters older women.

'Fine, as far as I know. I haven't seen him yet. He only drove down last night.' I deliberately left Nick to greet his father alone. They take a little time to slot into each other's orbits, and it takes longer in the presence of a third party.

'He must have been so worried,' Mother says.

'I expect he still is.'

My mother makes a *tsk tsk* noise, as if she didn't want to hear me say that. Having at first written Nick off – or so it felt to me – she seems now to have written him in so firmly that any doubt on my part is to be regarded as melodramatic.

It's nearly seven; time to walk the two hundred yards down the High Street to the Napoli restaurant. Both my mother and Nick's father are unadventurous eaters – with different limited dietary ranges – but everyone can find something they like in an Italian restaurant. We're booked for seven o'clock because Paul eats early at home and his digestive juices start without him if they're not fed on time, which he says is uncomfortable.

We arrive at the restaurant to find him and Nick already here, a bottle of Valpolicella open and well-started on the basil-green tablecloth in front of them.

Paul rises the instant he sees us. He is of that generation. Nick rises a split second later. I can tell that father and son have already made their connections; I sense invisible threads between them.

I kiss Paul, and he squeezes my shoulder. My heart heaves; I love this man almost as much as his son. He is a couple of years off seventy, still with a straight spine and a firm grasp. We don't see eye to eye about everything but practically never argue. He would let a point go, in any case, rather than offend in the pursuit of it. He is the product of a gentler, more decent, better mannered age. A gentleman. He has been devastated by Nick's illness. All his life he has done the right things, for his parents, his country, his wife and children, and he doesn't deserve the suffering he's recently had to endure. Three years ago, on the brink of his eagerly awaited retirement, his wife – Nick's mother – died, with brutal abruptness. She had been Paul's lifelong partner; they met when they were both only twenty-one. And just as his face, in repose, was regaining tone and life again, he learns that Nick, his only son, has cancer. Of course he doesn't burden anyone. His distress hardly shows, except in photographs – I've seen a couple from this summer – when his face flesh looks collapsed again, as it did after his bereavement, and on the phone, when he clears his throat and drops his voice and uses his pharynx, not his chest, to draw breath.

Tonight however he is in good form: immediately

warm, solicitous, fatherly, to us all. Taking our orders, pushing us to indulgence, acting as generous host. This suits my mother; she is aglow with pleasure before she's touched the wine. It seems to suit Nick too; sometimes he bucks against his father's patronage, but he seems relaxed enough tonight. He looks tired – the shop has been ridiculously busy this week, with every other thirteen-year-old wanting a guitar for Christmas – but relaxed too. Maybe it's the red wine. It's a family drink, isn't it? Warm and benign and huggy while you're drinking it, and for quite a while afterwards; and even, perhaps, domestic in the way it clubs you to death much later in the night, for no reason at all.

My mother settles happily into the meal. She's always got on with Paul, as, on a superficial level, she gets on with everyone. She slots easily into whatever mood is prevailing, goes with the flow, and has no hidden sharp corners herself. She is good at small talk and enjoys complimenting others – tonight, while Nick is out of earshot replacing menus on the bar, she tells Paul what a handsome son he has. She knows parents love hearing their offspring praised. Paul says, 'Bettina, dear,' with a fluffing laugh, a little embarrassed but also pleased, not because he believes the compliment (though he probably does) but because he appreciates that she is trying to please him. And I wince both at my mother's remark – I bet she says it to every man with a son, unless the son is undeniably three-headed – and at hearing Paul say her name, though I know its curvy girlishness suits her. But at least she hasn't said how proud Paul must be of Nick – another of her favourite compliments – which would be painfully inapt, just at present.

Before dessert (they do a wonderful nut-and-honey *figliata* I save room for) my mother goes off to the Ladies. This is another reason for choosing the Napoli – they have an excellent powder room. My mother will not eat – or indeed spend any time at all – in an establishment whose toilet facilities are unknown or of – in her view – a gruesome standard. That's why she used the station Ladies, of course. She hates the cramped, unisex train ones, and knows that the station facilities are acceptable. Lavatories are important to my mother. They are, she insists, to most women of her age. It is, she says, one of the great unmentioned facts of life. While she's gone Paul, who is on my right, takes my hand and presses it on to the green tablecloth.

'Nick looks splendid,' he says. 'But you're thinner. You mustn't let him wear you out.'

'I've been running a lot.' I'm brisk, brushing it aside. It's the truth, anyway.

'She should start a rickshaw business,' Nick says. A joke, but he knows what makes me run, so it's an acknowledgement too.

'You must look after her, Nick.' Paul's eyes entreat the two of us. He's had several glasses of wine. 'Please, look after each other.'

'Shut up, Dad,' says Nick, but so softly that it means: you don't need to tell us that.

A silence falls over us, during which my mother reappears. She stops in front of the table and throws her hands up.

'A camera!' she cries. 'That's what we need. Look at you!'

We immediately pull away from each other, as you do when you're suddenly self-conscious. But for once, although I don't think of my mother as the most perceptive of people, she's right. Even from a distance, trotting across the carpet towards us, she recognized an intimate moment. I'm impressed. It means she must have been looking at us. Not simply on social autopilot, but actually noticing us. And, to give her her due, she didn't mind not being part of the moment. She didn't seem to mind at all.

It was, altogether, a good evening. The best of the holiday, really. We spent Christmas Day as a foursome at Nick's cottage – I cooked, he washed up, Paul and my mother made the coffee – and it was pleasant, but the day itself is always a let down. How can it not be, with such a build-up? You've bought everything you need, unwrapped everything you've been given, eaten everything put in front of you, and everyone's shut away in their private home-based festivities and . . . that's it. Big deal. Of course it's more fun with children.

The best Christmas I've had, as an adult, was the one spent with Nick's sister and her family. But this year especially I wanted the holiday over. There's a milestone feel to dates like Christmas. They stick out like great solid obstacles that time has to slow down for, to heave itself over. Not what you want when you're waiting for time to slip away, to disappear while your back's turned. While you're notching up days, weeks, months. The further we get from last June, the more hope we're allowed.

Chapter 5

Malignant melanoma. It sounds wilful, doesn't it? Wilfully malicious.

And yet, what is a cancer? Just a bundle of multiplying cells. That's all. Cells that are, in essence – literally in essence – yourself. There is no attack from outside, no alien invasion, no evil, exterior force at work. Cancer is, simply, a bodily betrayal.

I cannot easily visualize a cancer cell. When I try, I come up with either a tiny, warped disc or an amoeba-like organism, with invading jelly-arms. When Nick was in hospital he was told by another patient to try visualization as a way of defeating cancer: to create pictures in his head of cancer cells, and imagine his body, represented by other, good-guy cells – using whatever imagery appealed – destroying them. He saw cancer cells differently to me: as powder-fine, lead-metal spheres – microscopic death stars – and imagined an army of pac-men, like in the computer game, coursing through the vessels of his body, munching up the spheres. He didn't think the idea silly; it gave, he said, curious satisfaction.

When you look up *malignant* and *cancer* in the dictionary, this is what you get:

> **Malignant** disposed to do harm; actuated by great hatred; tending to cause death, or to go from bad to worse. *Esp. cancerous.*
> **Cancer** the genus to which the edible crab belongs; a constellation (the crab); a sign of the Zodiac; any malignant new growth or tumour. Properly, a carcinoma or disorderly growth of epithelial cells which invade adjacent tissue and spread via the lymphatics and blood vessels to other parts of the body; any corroding evil.

I will go for 'actuated by great hatred' and 'disorderly growth'.

When you die of cancer, your death notice in the newspaper says: *after a long illness, bravely borne*. Everyone who has cancer, it seems – or everyone who dies of it, anyway – bears it bravely.

There is no good time to receive bad news. But some times are better than others. Sometimes one isn't prepared at all; not even contemplating the possibility. I swept into the shop to meet Nick like the lash of the

February rain outside, and my first words were unforgivable. Celia had just left, and Jason was up the road buying cakes from Batemans.

I snapped, completely unreasonably, 'How can anyone need more than fifteen bloody lessons?'

Nick stared at me – I thought he looked guilty, God help me, I didn't recognize terror – and said, 'I've got a lump.'

I said, 'Oh shit.' And a terrible thought flashed across my mind. A purely momentary thought. Just a crazy association of ideas, I'm sure, because I'd been thinking uncharitable thoughts about Celia, and they got attached to Nick's words. The terrible thought was that Celia somehow knew, that this was why she was still having lessons, that what she really wanted, in the furtherance of some silly, romantic, esoteric quest, was to seduce a dying man.

Then my thoughts went to pieces and we're sitting here together now in the shop, two pole-axed brains with not a coherent thought between us. Jason has just returned and been told the news – because he saw our faces and instantly said, 'Hey, you guys, what's wrong?' – and he's made everyone a cup of tea to go with the eight cakes he's bought. Two éclairs, two cream doughnuts and four custard slices. Cake eating, I'm afraid, is a vice he has caught from me. Nick can't eat. But I can, I discover. I've rammed the two doughnuts down already.

The lump is on Nick's shin. The shin of his bad leg.

He can't decide if it is freemoving or attached to the bone below. It's certainly not attached to the skin. He has rolled up his trouser leg to show us and I have felt it. It is the size of a large pea but not so spherical. Flatter. It's not tender; there's no feeling in it at all.

Jason is indignant. Nick is not allowed to be ill again. Heroes are not to be revealed as vulnerable. 'You've banged yourself, man,' he insists. 'That's nothing, that is. Hey, you've clocked yourself.'

This is possible. When he said it, my head nodded in agreement. Trouble is, Nick can't remember banging himself. Bangs on shins are usually painful. Memorably painful. On the other hand, it is the sort of uninteresting, thickened-flesh lump that, on anyone else, would not immediately suggest cancer. But at the hospital they said: *anything unusual.* It suggests cancer to us, because it is unusual, and because we're terrified of lumps.

Whatever, there's certainly been a growth of disorder here. Even the people on the street outside the shop look fragmented. The rain on the window glass distorts them. Hundreds of grotesque Picasso people have invaded our town.

Nick wants to stay at the shop because it's a way of using up time. It is part of the malignancy of the illness that the lump has been discovered on a Saturday afternoon, so he'll have to wait until Monday to ring the hospital. I don't know what I'll do over the weekend now; I can hardly remember what plans I had. Nothing that can't be jettisoned to fit in with Nick.

I stay with him all weekend. At night after we've made love – which we refuse to be frightened out of, though both nights I'm too tense to climax – we lie side by side in the darkness, awake but unspeaking; there's nothing to say. We touch at hip and foot. It is inadvisable to think at night, because darkness takes the brakes off and it's possible to accelerate to a state of panic that can be broken only by getting up, going downstairs, putting the light on and practising slow breathing. A substance or technique that produced instant unconsciousness would make its inventor a fortune. I desire this substance not for myself, but for Nick. I refuse to sleep until he does. I refuse to leave him alone. But it can take a long time. On the Sunday night when, at last, I hear his breathing change, I slip out of bed and take one of the four sleeping pills left over from when he first came out of hospital. On the bottle is written *Not on consecutive nights*. Nick says they don't work, but I disagree. The capsule is large and green and bullet-like, and achieves exactly what it is supposed to.

Thank God for work. Thank God Francine hustles. Thank God she leaves everything to the last minute, so on Monday I find I've six pages of organic farming information to write up in clear English and send to a dozen prospective sponsors by the end of the week. And this on top of all my other work: the petition forms still pouring in which have to be checked and counted, replies to ad hoc enquiries to be composed and typed – we're in all the environmental directories, so get inundated with school project requests – missing money to be tracked down across Europe, bundles of leaflets to be packed up and sent off, and articles to be photocopied from last week's newspapers. The day is passing quickly. Nick rang at ten this morning to say his consultant would see him at three, and he promised to ring me here if he got home before five.

But it's quarter to now and he hasn't rung. *Why? Has he been admitted? Are they operating? Is the news too awful to break over the phone?* Every time I think these thoughts, some organ just below my solar plexus takes a nosedive into my abdomen. I hate the physical symptoms of terror. To face terror you need to be fit; not doubly assailed, tormented by mind and body.

At five I leave work, and by now I'm angry as much as anxious. Or rather, my anxiety has become so acute that it has metamorphosed into anger. Anger is much more manageable. And it is justifiable. I don't believe Nick couldn't have rung by now.

I set off to drive straight to his cottage. No calling in at the flat first to change. But at the main road junction at the edge of town an extraordinary impulse hits me. Just for a split second, as I hesitate at the junction before crossing, I am tempted to turn right, away from the cottage, away from my flat, away from our town and what is happening to us here. I don't do it, but the fact that I thought it, if only for a micro-second, makes a cold sweat prickle my armpits.

A couple of minutes later I'm pulling up behind the Zodiac. Nick is here. He has a phone. He could have lifted it. Sod him.

The front door is open. Nick is becoming very careless; someone will steal his guitars one day. He is peeling potatoes in the kitchen.

'Well?' I don't mean to sound aggressive, but that's how it comes out.

Nick shrugs. 'They've taken a biopsy.' His smile is strained. 'I go back Thursday, two-thirty.' He pauses, and then says, 'He didn't say it might be. He didn't say it couldn't be. He was . . . noncommittal.'

'Oh shit.' Poor Nick. My anger is instantly transferred to the doctors, the hospital, the system. How can it take three days to look down a microscope? Don't they realize the urgency? It's the malignancy at work again, stretching the suffering out. Three more days of this.

I slump into the kitchen chair. Nick turns back to the potatoes. I hear the scrape of his knife. The splosh of water. Then he lifts his head.

'D'you want to come with me?' He hasn't turned. His expression is in the back of his head. 'On Thursday.'

He's asking me to go with him. He's admitting to fear. This is one of those moments that I'm meant to rush up to him, cradle him, comfort him. Why doesn't it happen? Because I refuse to do it. Because it would be giving in.

I say, 'Yes, sure, if you'd like me to,' as if, well, it isn't such a big thing. That's how he asked. *D'you want to . . .?* he said. Not, *I want you to . . .*

Nick nods over the sink. Half of me longs to get up, shout something, throw something, grab hold of him, hug him to me, break the glass between us. The other half hisses no, no, don't, stay put, stay cool; that's how the hobgoblins get in.

But I stay with Nick all week, although it feels strange. Before, when he was ill, there was a practical point to it. I was doing jobs for him. He needed physically looking after. Now, he can do his own cooking and housework, and I am simply here, a presence, my purpose undefined. Why am I here? To take his mind off things? To show solidarity with him? To protect him? To make the most of him? To be held on to at night? I don't know; but not being here would be desertion.

Everything is tainted with fear. The taste of it hits me a second after I wake in the morning. It is a constant distraction. It infects every conversation. To fill the time after work, while Nick is at the Playhouse, I run. I run into town, towards the lights. I hold a lit torch for the first and last half mile. I stick new reflective tape on the shoulders and back of my jacket and the heels of my running shoes; cars are a real danger on these dark unpavemented lanes. The weather is miserable too, wet and cold; the raw winds make my lungs hurt. Nick, when he's not at the shop or the Playhouse, strums Muriel incessantly. He doesn't play tunes. He needs to occupy his mind as well as his fingers, so he sets himself technical tasks. He explores the different ways of playing chords. On a guitar most notes can be found on several strings, and one combination can sound subtly different to another. He spends hours and hours experimenting with his left hand, and listening.

Toby the cat is not at all well. His stomach is now grotesquely distended, his shape asymmetrical. I cannot believe his deterioration at this time is fortuitous, and watching him afflicts me with creeping horror. On Wednesday morning, for the first time, he refuses his food. He stands over the bowl, dribbling a thin trail of saliva as if he wants to eat, but then plods away. His marmalade coat is clumped and has lost its shine. Nick and I both cuddle him as often as possible, and he can still purr.

That night in bed, in a semiconscious state, drifting in and out of sleep – it's the night before the hospital appointment, our last night of not knowing – I imagine some sort of terrible pact between Toby and Nick. Or, no, it's between Toby and the cancer. And I want to shout out, to warn Toby: *but the cancer's malignant, it hates us, you can't trust it . . .*

I go to work Thursday morning but return at lunch-time. It's a fifty-minute car journey to the hospital. We go in the Golf because the hospital car park is a maze and the Zodiac is so difficult to manoeuvre in tight spaces, but Nick drives. This is unusual; normally, because he dislikes travel – especially deadlined travel – he hands over responsibility for joint journeys to me, which includes the driving. But today he says he wants the distraction of doing something on the journey.

On the drive I try to imagine what the return journey might be like but the effort is beyond me. There is a solid wall, as wide as the eye can see and stretching upwards to infinity, between now and then.

The outpatient department is at the other end of the hospital from the inpatient entrance. Nick has been here before but I haven't. There are automatic glass doors that because of the volume of human traffic are constantly sucking in and out. I think they're dangerous; someone running fast out of the hospital could easily smash into them.

Inside the grey and red foyer Nick registers at the desk and is sent to the main waiting room. What follows is a sophisticated form of torture. Someone calls his name, and I think, *this is it,* but it isn't, it's just a request for him to get up, walk down a stretch of corridor, and sit down somewhere else. I accompany him; in this way we visit three waiting rooms. The final one has the consultant's door at the end, with the doctor's name in gold written on it. I won't be following in there; Nick will hear his fate alone.

While we wait we speak occasionally but say nothing, and have difficulty hearing each other. When I say something to Nick he focuses on me with such over-concentration that my throat aches and I want to kill someone.

At 3.15, three quarters of an hour after the appointment time, a nurse finally calls him. He jumps up, doesn't look back at me, and walks to the open door. It closes behind him.

I get up. I cannot sit and wait. The last hour has felt like forever. Time only advances when you do something. I walk round the corner from the waiting room and start pacing the corridor; the flooring is grey thermoplastic tiles which make the soles of my shoes squeak. Walking away from the consulting room my pace is brisk and urgent; in the return direction my footsteps are stickier, more faltering. I am terrified of the consulting room door, that rectangle of veneered wood; of the moment when it will open, and someone will come out and say, 'Excuse me, are you with Nicholas Baker . . . would you like to come in too . . . ?' I wonder, suddenly, whose idea it was for him to bring me. Isn't that what they tell you, when they may have to break bad news . . . *bring someone with you*?

I look at my watch. He's been in there for more than six minutes. What can they be talking about, if there's not a problem, that takes more than six minutes? Nothing can be worse than this: the state of not knowing. Even, surely, knowing the worst. You cannot accommodate to desperate hope. The world teeters on a razor edge between the brightest bright and the darkest dark. They're suffocating us. I haven't got enough air. I feel faint . . .

Then the door opens, and a nurse comes out. She is smiling at someone behind her. Who is Nick. I hear her say, loudly, 'Well, that's good news, isn't it?' and I see Nick's head nod. He looks like a child overwhelmed by adult munificence. I catch his eye and he organizes his face so it grows up again. His smile is almost bashful.

He walks up to me, grasps my hand very tight, and leads me away.

'So what was it?' I ask. My feet have stopped making a noise on the tiles. Because I'm floating above them, of course.

Nick says, 'He's not sure. Local trauma, probably. Not cancer, anyway.' He squeezes my hand. 'Jason was right.'

'We must ring him,' I say. We don't need to tell anyone else. No one else knows. Not Francine, not Nick's father. Not my mother. Jason's anxiety, such as it is, doesn't burden or frighten us. We can control it. He is our creature.

Nick rings him from the payphone in the hospital foyer. It's one of those perspex umbrella booths and I can see his expression while he's talking. His face splits into an eye-crinkling grin at something Jason says. I vote Jason our lucky mascot. He had faith. He stood up to the cancer. If he were here, I'd hug the boy till he gasped.

I drive on the return journey and I swear it takes half the time of the outward trip, even though we stop at an out-of-town Asda to pick up a litre of red wine. Why does agony slow time down, and euphoria speed it up? It seems most unfair.

When we get back to the cottage we are stupifyingly tired, but also ravenously hungry. Unlike me, Nick loses his appetite under stress; he hasn't eaten properly for days. I dig two pepperoni pizzas out of his freezer. The packets say that each serves four but they lie. I half cook them, to defrost them, and then add even more cheese and mushrooms. In my freezer at home I have a dairy cream cake that I'm getting flashes of, but it's too much bother to go into town and get it, and, anyway, it wouldn't go with red wine.

Toby won't eat his supper. He may have been sick in our absence too. The hair round his mouth smells of bile. I recognize it as the stench of cancer and know he's kept his pact with it. After we've eaten Nick picks him up and keeps him on his knee all evening. But he seems to make no connection between the cat's illness and his own; his manner is just normally tender and compassionate, like anyone about to lose an old feline friend.

Before we go up to bed he lifts the cat up on to his chest, strokes his tufty spine gently, and says he's going to ring the vet in the morning; Toby's time has come.

Immediately I say, 'I want to go with you.' I know there is a late-afternoon surgery. 'Make it after five. Please.'

Nick nods, and puts his head down to the cat. 'Ah, Toby, Toby,' he says. But it is a sighing, comfortable sadness. No overtones, no weight of significance behind it.

At work the next morning Francine comes into the office to do some photocopying of paperwork for her divorce solicitor, and I tell her that the real reason I took a half day yesterday was because we had a little scare at the beginning of the week and Nick had to go to the hospital to get the result of a biopsy on his shin. But the results were negative, and everything is fine.

I have put it lightly, but Francine still halts on her way to the copier and stares at me. Her eyes are horrified. Unlike Jason, her reactions are not controllable. She has the life experience to grasp the truth behind words.

'You should have told me. You must have been

desperate all week. My God, you poor things. What a nightmare.'

'Less at work than anywhere else,' I assure her. 'I'm so glad you're a hustler.'

'What d'you mean?' Francine is instantly side-tracked from her sympathy into defensiveness. 'You're the one who hustles.'

I laugh. 'No wonder we get so much work done.'

She is only partially mollified. 'You mustn't let me bully you. If that's what I'm doing.'

'I said I liked it,' I insist. 'I'm not complaining.'

'Well. Next time, whoever's the hustler, you mustn't suffer alone.' Francine moves on to the photo-copier but then stops again and sighs. She certainly doesn't believe in suffering alone herself. She waves the papers in her hand dispiritedly. 'Hustling's what Lionel's doing now, over the divorce. He ignores all my solicitor's requests, and bombards her with his own. He wants to see millions of documents. She's talking of retaliating with a court order to stop him moving his assets abroad. He will be *furious* if she does that.' She nods to herself. 'I mustn't be frightened of him. That's how he gets his way. By intimidation. Nobody dares call his bluff – we all hate conflict so much. Useless against someone who thrives on it.'

She lifts the photocopier cover. Underneath there's a newspaper neatly folded on the glass.

'Yours, I presume,' she says, passing it back to me.

I have no memory of photocopying any articles yesterday. I turn the paper over. It's the local rag. Someone has been photocopying an article about the Playhouse. No. The picture above it. It is a shot of Nick. Well, Nick and others. A photo of one of the town rock groups, the one Jason belongs to, in the Playhouse rehearsal rooms. Jason is on drums, a boy called Ricky on bass, his friend Simon lead guitar, and a boy whose name I forget singing. Nick is standing alongside on the right, playing his steel slide guitar, a beautiful silver instrument with flower-burst sound holes. They appear to be actually mid-number; the singer is mouthing straight at camera and Simon and Ricky are turned to Nick, grinning at him above their instruments. I know what is going on: a three-way guitar conversation. Nick holds his guitar much lower than the others and looks totally locked into the exchange. Music is a group activity; he has to listen, provoke, wait, respond. He seems unaware of the camera. He's a musician, not a performer. He's never liked the front of stages, where he's out of visual contact with co-players; he's the guitarist who's one of the team, even for his solos, when the blended line-up makes you wonder, just for a moment, where the clear, power notes are coming from.

Francine stares at the photo over my shoulder. 'Must be Celia's. She's got very keen on the guitar. Have you heard her? I'm impressed.'

Why does Celia want photos of Nick? How dare

she. No, let's be reasonable. He's her teacher. He used to be in a group, whose photo she has – or had – on her bedroom wall. She must admire him. Why shouldn't she want a photo of him? Why am I so hung up on Celia?

We discover at lunch-time why she has made the copy. She pops into the kitchen just as Francine is heating up soup. She is wearing a pale blue angora sweater. I can truthfully say that I have never before, in real life, seen anyone wearing an angora sweater. It gives her torso a fuzzy, ethereal outline. She drops two slices of wholemeal bread into the toaster.

'You left your picture on the photocopier.' Francine nods at the kitchen table, where she's put the newspaper.

Celia stares at her, then at the paper, and blushes. She actually blushes.

Francine doesn't say *Why were you copying that?* but the question hangs in the air. She is smiling as she stirs the soup; I suspect that she's enjoying discomforting her daughter.

Celia murmurs, 'I was writing to Bella. News, you know.' She shrugs.

Bella, I seem to recall, is one of her university friends. I imagine Celia's handwriting, the rounded, breathy, girly words that will go with the photocopy. *This is him, the one on the right. He used to be a rock guitarist, still is, really. I hang around his shop all the time. We get on really well . . . I know he likes me . . . he has this boring girlfriend but I'm working on it . . . you know me . . .*

A violent sensation attacks me. So violent I have to start swallowing, trying to gulp it away. It is a new fear, sprung fully armed and roaring from a hidden corner of my mind. I put my hand over my mouth. I re-live the feeling of that moment four days ago, driving to Nick's cottage, when I experienced the impulse to run away from him. It is myself I am afraid of. Of what I might do, or what I might want to happen. I've said it to myself before: nothing is sacred now. Everything is up for grabs. Do I want Celia to seduce Nick? Or Nick to seduce her? What a lunatic idea. What a mad, destructive, disorderly idea. Why should I want that? Why would I want to lose him?

In the evening Nick and I don't bother with the cat box. Toby is too weak to argue about a car trip, and in the vet's surgery he sits quietly on Nick's lap. The lady the other side wants to make friends with him. 'Hello, pussy,' she says, and clucks her tongue at him. 'Are we poorly?'

Nick says, 'Yes,' without adding that Toby is so poorly that he's going to be put down for it. I am excruciated. Another waiting room. This one has thermoplastic tiles too. How can Nick be so calm, so blind to the parallels? He is either more rational than I, or better at protecting himself. He does, of course, have more need to protect himself. It has to be harder to be him than to be me, so maybe he simply has to be tougher. I expect that's it. He can't afford to indulge in fantastic notions.

And yet I can't help my feelings. I am convinced that we should be thanking Toby, that in some way he has protected Nick. Whatever my brain tells me, I know, in my heart, that his cancer saved Nick. That Toby took the evil on himself.

Oh, superstition is an insidious master. It gets between the brain cells, into the logic circuits, and forces them apart.

A male face appears at the door and says, 'Toby Baker?' Nick rises. In this practice pets take on the surnames of their owners. There is something touching about the custom.

I follow Nick to the examination room. The vet is a bearded man of about forty, with big hands and very short fingernails. He looks enormously strong, as if he could wrestle a recalcitrant bull to its knees. I know these surgeons do a lot of large animal work. Nick puts Toby down on the plastic-coated examination table.

'He's stopped eating,' he says. 'I think he's begun to suffer.'

The vet nods, says, 'Hello, Toby, old man,' and gently runs his huge hands over Toby's sides. Toby gives a low, quiet cry.

'It is very advanced.' He considers a moment and then says, 'I could, if you like, give you something to try . . .?'

'No.' Nick shakes his head.

'The end of the road, then, is it?' The vet strokes Toby's ears. Toby actually pushes his head against those huge fingers. I nearly make a small noise.

The vet looks up at us and says, 'D'you want . . .?'

'To stay?' asks Nick. 'Yes.'

'Right.' The vet gives Nick a form to sign and turns away to prepare his syringe. Nick signs, then picks Toby up and holds him against his chest. He strokes a finger under his chin and kisses him, lightly, on the top of his head. Then hands him to me. 'Jess. Say goodbye.'

I take Toby and drape him against my shoulder. I want him to purr in my ear, as I rock him this way and that, but he doesn't. It is time, I tell him silently. If a cat can't purr, he's better off dead.

I put him back on the table. Nick holds him still while the vet clips fur from his front leg, so he can find the vein for his needle. Then he slides the needle in. Toby seems to unravel in Nick's arms. Just lays his head down, and stops living. He seems suddenly a much smaller cat, as if life occupies space. Lying on his side, the lump in his flank is very obvious. He seems a much smaller, and much more diseased cat.

The vet slips out of the room. He's giving us a moment to say farewell. To a dead body.

'I'm going to leave him here.' Nick's eyes are wet,

but his voice is steady. 'They cremate them. They say it's dignified.'

I have no garden. Nick's is waterlogged at the moment. Toby would hate cold wet clay. Like all cats, he loved heat. His tail-fur caught ablaze once when, in an ecstasy of log-fire-revelling, he brushed too close to the unguarded flames.

The vet returns and we thank him, and leave. Nick pays at reception, in front of the roomful of other pet owners, and I am convinced that everyone knows that Toby is dead. They saw us come in with an old ginger cat and we are leaving without him. The atmosphere is sober and sympathetic. I refuse to meet anyone's eye; I mustn't crack, just yet.

Nick drives me back to my car, which I left outside his cottage. He's got a gig tonight, helping out one of the town groups whose lead guitarist is laid up with tonsillitis. It's just a low-profile pub gig, and the group are talented and good company; any other night and I might have gone along too. But tonight I need to be on my own.

I drive home and let myself into my dark, empty flat. I haven't slept here since last Friday. It is at least warm; the shop underneath and the flats either side insulate it. I would normally go for a run, feeling as I do, but tonight decide not to. A very great pressure has built inside me and I need to let it build. I want to express, tonight, not suppress.

I have to be on my own because I cannot explain to

Nick how I feel. I can't tell him that it feels safe to mourn for Toby, because he is only a cat. I can't tell him that he has become a receptacle for my grief.

I let the pressure mount further while I make myself scrambled egg and toast and Marmite. Invalid food. I carry it on a plate into the sitting room, turn on the television, and curl up in my big armchair. An Australian soap is on; I can't immediately tell which one. I watch it without following what is happening.

The only disadvantage of scrambled egg is that it is too easy to eat – it's gone in five minutes. I put the plate aside. I need to release the pressure now, so I close my eyes, tip my head back against the chair cushion and visualize Toby's little ginger body on the vet's table. I stare at the image, and realize that he has shrunk around his cancer. His own flesh has fed it.

I start to wallow in sentiment. I remember him across my shoulders, his clinging, kneading claws, his bony body vibrating with pleasure. How his purr was the most comforting sound in the world. My throat is stiffening. It's working, I'm breaking, the tears are coming.

What a relief; a blessed outpouring. I should cry more often. I used to cry in front of Nick but since his illness there's been only one occasion when I've succumbed – that worm-eating day back in November when I was so depressed and cried in his car. Normally I protect him from any distress I feel, because he needs a partner who is strong, who can cope with anything. But even the strong need a night off. I'm nearly smiling as I cry. Toby, Toby, I mouth, dear cat. We will miss you.

Chapter 6

My first question is: who cares – really cares – whether you live or die? And the answer I've come up with? Fewer people than you'd think. And definitely fewer than if I'd asked myself the question a year ago. Not that, in unthreatened circumstances, it's a question one tends to ask. But I have been thinking. There are your parents, if they're still alive. Your brothers and sisters, if you've got any. Your children, if you've got any. Your close friends, ditto. Your partner, if you've got one. These are all people whose lives overlap with yours. Whose lives would be profoundly altered by your absence. Who, whatever the ambiguities of their feelings for you – and not all parents like their children, not all brothers love their sisters – nonetheless will care what happens to you. They can't help it; they're locked into your influence, you're locked into theirs. But the others: colleagues, acquaintances, minor friends. Well, some would be shocked. Some would be appalled. Some would be sad. Genuinely. But there's a difference. Their emotional universe would not be irrevocably altered. They would not be bereaved.

Nick has his father, his sister and me. I'm doubling as partner and close friend. Three people. He has countless friendly acquaintances, fellow musicians he plays with, staff at the Playhouse, and a small number of others that he refers to as good friends, but they're mostly from the old days and they all live counties – often countries – away. It's a self-delusion to say you're close friends with someone you never actually see. Jason should be counted. Jason is not a true friend – the relationship isn't equal enough for that – but he does love Nick, and his life would be affected, practically and emotionally, if Nick died. Otherwise . . .

It makes you feel like rushing off and having babies.

And my second question is: is there a limit to our capacity to care? At what point, if only to protect ourselves, do we snuff the care candle out?

Human beings, we're told, are designed to react well to trauma. We cope, under acute stress, extraordinarily well. Biologically all the right things happen. We very rarely drop dead with shock, as some living creatures do. Birds, small mammals. Instead we rise to the catastrophe. Our bodies surge with adrenalin, our capabilities soar to super-human levels, we find resources to achieve the near-impossible. Psychologically, too, we excel. We react, under acute stress, both self-protectively and altruistically. Unlike animals, threatened grown-up humans will save the lives of other grown-up humans. Even complete strangers. Under acute stress, the human animal can be magnificent.

Often the problems seem to come afterwards. When the acute danger is over, or is perceived as receding. When the stress drops to low-key. When the adrenalin tails off to a trickle, or is exhausted altogether. Human beings may be good at stress. But better at the short cataclysmic event, perhaps, than the long haul.

What was the question? *Is there a limit to our capacity to care?* I don't know. But if you don't snuff the care candle out, I think, eventually, it would burn out anyway.

Today, the first Monday in April, two significant events are occurring. The first concerns Nick. Even as I sit in my office at work, Nick is less than two miles away at his shop being interviewed by an enthusiastic young male journalist from a Sunday newspaper colour magazine, for an article to be published next weekend. What has happened is that, for the second time already this year, the number-one chart hit is a cover version of an eighties song and, in this latest instance, the song is 'Lords of the Universe'. The contemporary pop and rock scene has been somewhat retrospective of late, and the songs of groups long defunct have been dredged out, or revamped by newcomers, to see what luck they have. The Sunday newspaper, which is trying to enliven its image and appeal more to the young, is planning an article – so we understand – along the lines of *Where are they now?* The *they* in question being members of the original groups.

The journalist assigned to this article must have been fifteen or so at the time Nick's group was popular, but he doesn't seem to have been very clued up, musically speaking, at that age. (Possibly he went to public school and was into Perry Como.) He has consequently had to do considerable research for the article, and it was while doing this that he came across reports of Nick's dramatic (in reality, over-dramatic) exit from the rock world, which he must have decided would make good copy. After establishing that Nick was still alive, still a musician of sorts, and still had contacts in the music business, he decided to start his article here. Nick, incidentally, as co-writer of 'Lords of the Universe' (he wrote the music, the singer the lyrics) is due to receive a not insignificant windfall from the song's current popularity. It's a fluke that the record's taken off; it's sung by a female indie group this time, and was produced initially not as a chart contender, but as the theme song for a series of vaguely hip BBC2 documentary programmes about 'the future of men', and the disappearance of traditional male roles. Which is, essentially, what the song is about. The deliberate irony – which one suspects was largely missed the first time round, by non-fans, anyway – has come to the fore. It is now clearly a song about ludicrous male pretension. *Lords of the Universe, masters of creation, fathers almighty* . . . The current version was released as a single by popular request and went straight to number one. It is being bought, I suspect, both by those who understand and admire the song's irony, and those who don't, and simply take the title and lyrics at face value. Like 'Stand by Your Man', which pleases everyone, for all sorts of contradictory reasons.

It is ten years since Nick was last interviewed, and that was only for a specialist guitar magazine. But he seems, oddly I think, to be looking forward to this interview. I say oddly because he has done fame, albeit in a shortlived way, and got the T-shirt (four, in fact, one for each tour) and surely has no ambitions in that direction. His inclination, these days, is more to avoid the limelight.

But perhaps he's just flattered. Why not? It's gratifying for him to see his song come round again, and for it to be more widely appreciated this time, with no effort on his part. It is his song – well, his and his co-writer's; why shouldn't he enjoy a little attention on the strength of it?

So that's happening at the shop. Here, at work, rather more domestic events are taking place. I have come in today to work, of course, but also to provide moral support to Francine, during one of Lionel's visits. I'm not sure if I'm chaperone or witness; whatever

Francine wants me to be, I suppose. I haven't seen Lionel yet, but I know he's here because I've seen his Range Rover in the drive. Doubtless I'd hear if Francine screamed for me. He's come in the Range Rover and not his Mercedes because the purpose of the visit is to remove various objects that Francine has agreed are his exclusively, and which are not fixtures, fittings or essential furnishings of the house. She is hoping to be awarded sole ownership of the property in the divorce settlement. Lionel does, after all, have a much larger house, nay, mansion, of his own near Oxford, plus half of their joint flat on the Embankment in London. (These people, as I've said, are way out of Nick's and my league.)

Francine is convinced that Lionel, being Lionel, will find some way during the visit to pull a fast one over her. Not because he's short of anything, or thinks he's getting an unfair deal, but just for the vindictive fun of it. She's hidden one or two favourite possessions in my office. At the back of my top drawer is a suede jewellery bag containing a number of pieces – none fabulously precious, except to her – inherited from her mother. And wrapped in a rug behind my towers of petition form boxes is the framed Wizard of Oz picture that used to hang in her bedroom when she was a child. I think it's an old print of a cinema poster. It shows Dorothy and her companions dancing up the yellow brick road towards an emerald-green horizon, while sinister black witch-silhouettes loom overhead. The colours are rich and still vivid. It is beautiful, but a frightening choice for a child's bedroom, I've always thought; she says it used to give her astonishing childhood dreams.

My feeling is that with these precautions Francine is overestimating Lionel's malevolence – or at least the extent to which it might be translated into actual mischief. There may be an element of counter attack here: *see how wicked you are, the measures I have to take.* Besides which, although jewellery could be slipped into a pocket, a three foot by two foot picture certainly couldn't. Although when I pointed this out Francine said darkly, 'He could damage it.' Most of what she is allowing him to take are items he came into the marriage with, or personal memorabilia. She's stacked most of it on the quarry tiles in the corner of her entrance hall. There are a couple of gloomy portraits of ancestors in flaking gilt frames, a tea chest containing a porcelain and gold-leaf dinner service that was last used at Philip's christening, a Jacobean carver chair which was Francine's present to him when they got married, and various ornaments some of which are valuable, but none of which she treasures. A few, she told me, she would have a right to argue over, but she's not going to. Save your powder, she has told herself. Don't exhaust yourself over trivia.

As far as I know, Lionel has arrived on his own. Francine told me that if he brought a mistress with him – *my assistant,* he would introduce her as, with a make-a-scene-if-you-dare smile – she would indeed dare, and make an embarrassingly noisy fuss. So far this morning I've heard nothing untoward. In fact the house seems unusually quiet. Lionel is taking Celia out for lunch later, but till then she is banished from the property – to give Francine the freedom to make scenes if she wishes, presumably.

I've just arranged myself sitting on the carpeted floor of the office, with a foot-high stack of completed petition forms in front of me – it is the most convenient place to sort nationalities into piles – when the door opens. A man comes in. This is Lionel.

He is a big man, but not fat. He has powerful shoulders, a barrel chest, a thick neck, close-cut white-grey hair, and tiny eyes. Tiny, intelligent, sperm-whale eyes. He should be the ugliest man in the world but he isn't. He is wearing a grey suit and exudes the confidence of a man who gives orders to God.

He says, smiling down at me, 'What a charming sight.'

I lift my top lip at him. I don't bother to get up. I'm not impressed by wealth or power or breeding. I have heard enough tales about him from Francine to keep him firmly midget-sized. Though he has a large nose, I realize, looking up at it. I hadn't noticed before. It's not unattractive on him, though it could be on someone who didn't admire himself as much as he does.

'You'll excuse me,' I say, 'I'm sorting petition forms.' Annoyingly, I find myself aware of the fact that the knees of my jeans are not particularly clean. Nor are my hands, which are grey with ink. Many of the forms are very poor photocopies.

He comes further into the room, looking delighted to be invading the office of a grovelling woman. His eyes – they're blue, or maybe green, hard to tell, they're so small and deepset – flick round the room. Demeter was his baby once. Before he got bored with it and moved back full-time to his bigger, more interesting and more lucrative babies. But I expect he still feels he has a right to snoop round the office.

'Looking for anything in particular?' I ask. I bundle a stack of Australian petition forms together. Names at the top catch my eye. Row upon row of Wombats and Joeys. Brian Wombat, address Billabong Creek, Didgeridoo. Sheila Joey, Eucalyptus Lodge . . . shit, a joker. I rip the form out from under the elastic band and scrunch it up. The one underneath looks all right.

'Just popped in to say hello,' Lionel says. 'To see how an old friend's doing.'

He must mean Demeter, not me. I get to my feet and start restacking the forms on to my desk for counting.

'Well, as you can see,' I say. 'We're definitely busy.'

Lionel laughs at me. With his mouth wide open, and the corners of his eyes at full crinkle. Patronizing creep. It's the sort of laugh that's meant to be flirtatious. *Ooh, you do disapprove of me, don't you?* Forcing complicity on me. I wonder what he'd do if I punched him on his large nose. Or in his possibly even larger balls.

'You look as if you want to hit me. My my.' He shakes his head in admiration. 'Bet you could deliver quite a punch, too. Still running are you? Still keeping fit?'

I sit down in my chair. The answer, I know, is not to argue. Not to fight. Not to secrete the scent of aggression. To Lionel, it is an aphrodisiac. He's a man who enjoys spunk in a girl. Who revels in the chase. To whom the chase is the main event. He does not, I'm sure, really desire me. Flirtation is simply a reflex. He is a classic, insatiable seducer.

But it is too late now to put him off by fawning over him or offering him sex on the desk. He'd guess it was a tactic.

I haven't bothered to answer his question but he hasn't noticed; he's spotted the rug-covered Wizard of Oz picture behind the cardboard boxes. He lifts the corner of the rug.

'She didn't want it getting muddled up with your pictures,' I say.

A distressed look clouds Lionel's face. I can't tell if it's genuine or put on for my benefit. It says *Does she really think I'm such an ogre?* A good thing he doesn't ask it aloud. My answer would have to be yes.

He tucks the picture up again and turns back to me.

'I have something for you. A farewell gift.'

'Don't be silly,' I say.

He doesn't like that. Being called silly. He touches his nose and for a moment it just looks big. No longer noble, or masterful.

'Jessica,' he says. 'Allow me, please.'

Jessica, eh? This is very forward of him. How many times have we met? Three, four times, at the outside? Practically everything we know of each other has been gleaned via a third party. The same third party. I wonder how Francine describes me?

'Think of it as something you can use in the business, if you like.' From the inside pocket of his suit jacket Lionel lifts out a white bone paperknife with a silver handle. He holds it across the palm of his hand. A quite charming object. One that I could imagine treasuring. I wipe the excess grime from my own palm off on my jeans and take it from him.

'It's lovely,' I say, sincerely.

He is pleased. His chest puffs out. 'It's yours. I thought you'd like it.' Then, in an overfamiliar act, he reaches out and wraps my fingers around it. There is something sensual, even erotic about the gesture. I don't pull away; that would acknowledge the undercurrent.

'Keep it safe now,' he says, detaching himself.

'Oh, I will.'

He lifts a farewell hand and backs away. I smile at him until the door closes, and then settle down in my chair. I want to chuckle. I don't think he properly comprehends my relationship with Francine. I don't think he knows that I have house-sat for her, that I have entered and am familiar with every room in her house and with their openly displayed contents. I stare down at the bone blade of the paperknife. I don't think it's ivory. But it looks uncomfortably close to it. He should have thought of that. Much too close to be of use in an environmental organization.

I put the knife to one side. After Lionel's left I'll give it back to Francine. I recognized it immediately, of course. It belongs on the pretty walnut desk in her bedroom. There is a silver inkwell to match.

In fact Francine goes out too, after Lionel's Range Rover departs, so I don't get the chance to give the knife back to her in person. I simply replace it on the bedroom desk during the afternoon. I assume that I will tell her about Lionel giving it to me right up to that moment. And then, leaving the bedroom, I wonder if I will. Francine would pretend to find it funny when, in truth, it's not. Underneath, she will be angry and upset. I would be telling her purely for my own satisfaction, displaying my determination to be on her side, by having no secrets from her. But I don't have to hurt her. Even if she's already noticed the knife's absence, I needn't tell her Lionel gave it to me. I could just say that he was fiddling with it when he came in to the office and left it with me. Yes, that's what I'll do. I realize I've been wanting to make a bigger deal of the episode than it deserves, and, I think in sudden gloom, I know why, too. I'm feeling on the edge of other people's dramas, and I don't like it, so I am exaggerating my role in them. Nick invited me to the shop for this morning's interview and I declined to go. Why? Not just because I knew Francine wanted me at work. I could have got out of that. But because I would definitely have felt on the edge there. The interview was about Nick's old life. His past was the *raison d'être*. I belong to his new life. His normal life. His real, still threatened life.

It's six days till Sunday: article publication day. Nick digs out old photos of himself, requested by the interview journalist, and sends them off, but gets the message back that the pictures the photographer took at the shop (I hadn't even known a photographer was present) are so good that they'd prefer to use them. But they've taken the liberty of copying his prints for possible future use. Nick says the interview was a hoot – his grin, that evening, belonged on a kid quarter his age – and has had no second thoughts about it. The prospect of his face on half a million Sunday breakfast tables spooks him not at all. Not even on Saturday night, in bed, when I try to frighten him with horror tales of the British press. It could be treachery, I warn him; sugar-coated words face to face, then the knife in, when his back is turned. But he only sniggers into my armpit.

The next morning he leaps out of bed soon after eight to go to the newsagent. He doesn't bother to get properly dressed; just pulls on his bedroom tracksuit trousers and his boots and runs down for his greatcoat. He thinks he's in one of the paper's lifestyle ads already. I remain in bed. He's back in ten minutes with an armful of newsprint.

'Got one each,' he says, throwing a wodge at me. He peels off his clothes and gets back into bed. There's something silly about us opening up identical colour supplements, sitting naked propped on pillows beside each other, but we do it anyway.

We find the article simultaneously. Hard to miss; there's a full-page photo of Nick. I am astonished. How long is this piece? Are they devoting full pages to everyone? I flick over; no, doesn't look like it. I turn back to the photo. Nick is outdoors in his greatcoat – the very one he's just taken off – leaning against the wing of the Zodiac. It's a colour photo, but without much colour in it. Mostly blacks and greys. Black car, black coat; even Nick's hair looks black, though in reality it isn't. The walls behind and the tarmac in front are grey. Grainy grey. White words across the top say *The One Who Got Away* and along the bottom, in smaller print, there's a quote. *'When you get a second chance, you know you've got to take control of your life.'* How very pompous, I think. But the picture is stunning. I am reminded how intensely photogenic Nick is. It's because he can hold any pose he's asked to without stiffening into it. Although he is not always a relaxed person, you'd never know from photographs of him. This is, clearly, a pose, but still manages to look just-captured. The spontaneous, off-guard, cinéma-vérité look.

The Nick of the photo is not the Nick I know. It is an earlier, vaguely familiar version of him. The media-friendly version, who has natural style and quiet charisma. I have a sinking suspicion that if I were a detached viewer of this photograph I might want more. And that an editor might understand this. The picture, I sense, is a threat.

I turn my attention to the text. I can tell, from the small snorting noises beside me, that Nick is already reading it.

The angle of the article isn't as I imagined. Not at all as we'd been led to expect. The subject matter seems to have narrowed from the general to the particular. Rather than a broadbased résumé of the careers of has-been rock musicians, this first page, at least, is exclusively about Nick. About one particular musician's life-story since the middle eighties. A musician who happens – almost coincidentally, one feels – to be co-writer of the current number one hit. It is an article not about music, or musicians, but about the search for personal fulfilment. It's about leaving rat-races and the oppressive demands of others, deciding what you want to do with your life, and organizing yourself to achieve it. It's about priorities. The details of Nick's day-to-day life are recounted. His shop, his work at the Playhouse with musicians and amateur groups. The occasional – very occasional, they should have said – session work at local recording studios. The article emphasizes that these are always local – ie, no further than Bristol – so he doesn't have the hassle of long journeys, or staying over. It tells us how, in his old rock-group days, Nick loved playing, but hated the rest of it. About how, at eighteen – even at twenty-two – it was impossible to say no to anything. But about how, after his electrocution, he learnt to value himself, and to perceive what he really wanted out of life; which wasn't a rock star's frenetic existence.

The article makes his life sound idyllic. Nick lives, we are told, in a small cottage on the outskirts of a thriving, unspoilt country town. The journalist claims to have been envious, impressed by the quality of small-town life: the lack of traffic jams or parking problems, the country-fresh air, the friendliness in shops, and the sheer pleasure – which he claims to have forgotten, living in London – of cruising small-town streets. He found two cheerful buskers in the clean, moneyed pedestrianized town centre, and no beggars.

Nick apparently has a royalty income of about £5,000 a year. I've no idea if this is correct. The article says he is going to at least double this with the current hit. (In fact, the impression is given that he has already benefited from it, which of course he hasn't. Royalty cheques dribble in over years; it's always jam tomorrow.) We are told that there is no distinction in Nick's life between work and play. He enjoys – more than enjoys – everything he does. He is as popular with the Chamber of Trade, who see his shop as a valuable town asset, as he is with the comprehensive school headmaster, who believes his Playhouse work keeps bored young men off street corners, as he is with the young men themselves. What a together, sorted, paragon. Even Jason's played along. He's quoted as saying: *Nick's the perfect employer. People and music come first. He's paying for me to learn the trumpet, you know.*

I flick the page over. God, the article runs half-way down the next page, too. I scan it quickly. It's of less interest. The journalist has finally picked up on his original brief, and is giving us the potted histories of other ex-rock-group musicians. But what's this? At the bottom there's another, much smaller, photo. Nick and Jason, outside the window of the shop. And in the open doorway stands Celia. Celia? What a cheek.

'How did she get in there?' I ask. 'Bloody hell.'

'She was around.' Nick says. 'The photographer suggested it.' His voice sounds dreamy. As if he's in a state of mild shock.

The article says Nick is single. That he lives alone.

No mention of a girlfriend. Just those quotes from little, pretty, disreputable-looking Jason, his assistant. His *assistant.* I look back to the first picture again; the Zodiac suddenly brings to mind a much more famously iconic vehicle.

'Batman and Robin,' I say. 'He probably thought everyone would assume you were gay, without her.' I put on a camp voice, with Jason's accent. '"He pays for my trumpet lessons, you know . . ."'

Nick gives a bark of laughter. 'You may be right.'

I lay the paper back. 'Did you know that this was going to be mainly about you?'

Nick shrugs. 'I could see the journalist was enthusiastic. How they angle things is up to them, isn't it? I knew there'd be a picture.'

'Huh.' I pick the paper up again and stare at it. 'So why didn't you mention me?' I've kept all petulance out of my voice. I think.

Nick doesn't reply for a moment. He lifts his head from his magazine and stares straight ahead. Then turns to me.

'I assumed,' he says, 'that you wouldn't want me to. That if I did, you would shout at me. That you would accuse me of turning you into an appendage.'

That shuts me up. I hunch down into my shoulders. Search around for another angle. I smack the page in front of me.

'This isn't you.'

'So?' Nick smiles. Anyone would think that it not being him was its main appeal. He's stopped sounding shocked now. He sounds exultant.

'Well . . .' I pull a scornful face. 'I mean. It's excruciating.'

'It's hilarious,' Nick says. 'Ridiculously hilarious.'

He's right, but I am too. Of course, this article is a fairy tale. There's no mention anywhere of the fact that Nick is recovering from cancer. No mention of the fact that he is travel phobic. That when he talks about the 'hassle' of travelling he means a lot more than that. That he is a big fish in a little pond because he couldn't cope with big ponds. I'm not criticizing him; big pond life would screw up most people. But the truth is that his present lifestyle is an escape. A retreat. Not a voluntary setting aside of anything he was once capable of handling.

I turn back to the beginning of the article and reread it. My eyes linger over the words *single* and *lives alone*. I've forgotten now who living apart was meant to benefit. I always seem to be here at the cottage these days. Once, Nick used to stay over at my flat as often as I stayed here. When was the last time? At least a month ago. I don't think he's stayed with me more than three times since he was ill.

'Why don't we live together?' I ask. I'm not suggesting that we should, I simply want the answer.

'Because you eat cakes and I don't.'

'You do.'

'Only when you're here. That's what I mean. I'd be elephantine.'

I drop the magazine back on to the duvet. I am unrestful to live with too, I know. I can't help it. My mother used to worry about it. 'You pace, Jessica,' she used to complain. 'When you get married, you won't be able to pace.'

But I don't pace any more because I run. You could marry someone who runs. Although there'd still be the cake incompatibility. But actually, now I've turned my mind to it, I think it was I who insisted on separate homes, not Nick. I'm sure we weighed up the pros and cons of living together, and there were a few pros, like savings on fuel bills and my mortgage, but there were a lot more cons, like not having your own bedroom and not being able to be as untidy as the mood took you, and arguing about who did what chores; and, of course, having a tame, domestic love life. It's always sexier to make love in someone else's bed, or on someone else's sofa, or someone else's carpet. If you live apart, one of you always has that advantage. We discussed all this, and I said we should stay separate, and Nick agreed. We said we'd review the decision if we wanted to have children.

Nick is deep in the magazine again. In fantasy land. That's what this is to him. I pick up my copy and flick through the rest of it. We never normally buy Sunday papers. They take too long to read and they're full of articles telling you how to live your life: what to eat, what to drink, what to wear, what to read, what to think. Or features about people who need publicity for some reason. They've just published a book, or starred in a film, and the feature is simply part of the hype. Readers will probably think Nick wants publicity: that he's cutting a new CD, or writing his autobiography, or, no, I'm missing the obvious – writing a life-style manual. There's a paradox here. An article about someone who is proud of having left the fame-fest, which nonetheless suggests – simply by its inclusion in the magazine – that he is eager to rejoin it.

As I skim the pages I am aware of my face pulling into a sneer. There's an article about holidays, and about how much trendier it is these days to holiday in Britain than abroad. There are several pictures of families looking active and windswept outside their British beach homes. Anyone would think no one had ever holidayed in Britain before. Anyone would think everyone could afford two homes. I flick over. The fashion page is about cardigans. How to look designer clad – in a cardy? – at a fraction of designer prices. Their *Loose Change* recommendation is a mauve lambswool cardigan costing sixty-five pounds. *Sixty-five pounds?* It's not even an attractive cardigan. It looks as if it might belong to one of my mother's pastel twin sets. But then, twin sets may well be in fashion now. I wouldn't know. I'm so out of touch.

I've remembered the real reason I don't read Sunday broadsheets. It's not because they're dictatorial, or obsessed with style trivia when other people are wrestling with real life and real death. It's because they make me feel panicky. Because I can't identify with the lifestyles they're reflecting. I feel left behind. And now Nick has leapt into their pages. Maybe he's trying to leave me behind too. Just now, that's what it feels like.

I tell him this over breakfast downstairs and he says, 'Twaddle.' And I know it is twaddle. I am projecting my feelings of marginality into everything. I even projected it into his store cupboard before we sat down. He is right, I thought, staring into the bleak recesses. Even my diet is off his map. He owns no peanut butter. No chocolate spread. No golden syrup. No jam, even. Only extra-bitter marmalade and Marmite. A hairshirt diet. How could we ever live together?

Soon after breakfast, at about eleven o'clock, the phone rings. I'm looking at the news section of the paper, with it spread out on the kitchen table. At least this section doesn't make me feel left behind; I keep up with news. I hear Nick sounding animated. I bet myself it's someone who's read the colour supplement piece. Nick talks for about ten minutes, and then comes to the kitchen door.

'Someone saw your picture?' I ask. He's leaning against the door jamb. How stylishly he strikes the attitude. How smug he looks.

'Robert. He wants me to do his afternoon show. Be his guest.'

'And?' Robert is an old friend. Well. A friend from the old days. Once a DJ. He now has an afternoon slot on national radio.

'I said yes, but I wasn't going to London. He says no problem, they'll use a Bristol studio.'

I stir my second cup of coffee. Nick doesn't move. He can see I'm thinking.

I put the teaspoon down. 'Are you trying to start things up again?'

Nick hesitates, but it's not because he doesn't understand what I mean.

'I don't think so.'

'Then what's this about?'

'It's just a radio show.' He sighs, pushes himself away from the door jamb and comes into the room. 'I don't know. You've only got one life.'

'I thought you quite liked your present life. I thought that was precisely what the article was about.'

'I do. I do. It's just . . .' He pours himself coffee from the jug. He waves a hand at me. 'But . . . maybe I should try, you know . . .'

'Try what?'

'Things. Different things.' He sits down. 'I'm just going on how I feel. There's no masterplan. I just feel . . .' His arms sweep the table, indicating something wide, expanding. 'Do things. Try things.' His expression urges me to understand. 'Come on, Jess, you know.'

*

At the time I raised an eyebrow. An *I'm not sure I do* eyebrow. But yes, of course I know. I'm being selfish. I'm resisting change. Telling people they shouldn't change. That they should stay frozen in time, as they are now, just as I like them. Maybe he could handle the big-time better than he could a decade ago. He was far too young for it then – Paul always said so: just a talented but immature kid. So why shouldn't he try again, while he's still talented, but now a mature man? Why shouldn't he spread his arms like that, why shouldn't he imagine moving out again into the world? What put him here in the first place, except his failures? Why shouldn't he want to opt out of them?

Because what, after all, despite his crappy, pompous, dishonest article, is so bloody wonderful about his life here?

Chapter 7

That's what cancer makes you do: rethink your life. Not immediately maybe; early on you're terrified that you're going to die any minute, and any kind of looking to the future is paralyzing. But, after a while, when you realize that no one dies instantly of cancer, and that even if it is going to kill you it's going to take its time over it, a reassessment, and then readjustment, takes place. It has to. When the old securities, the old givens of life, are shot apart, it's human nature to try to reassemble them. The rest of your life is concertinaed into a few years rather than decades, maybe, but it's still there, a viable length of time. Long enough to contain important experiences. Long enough to make changes. Long enough, usually, between crises, to function adequately in. People bring forward things they hadn't planned to do for a while. Or things they've been putting off, or just been too busy, or lazy, to get round to. That trip across the world to see relatives, or the Himalayas, or the whales of the Azores. That sailing boat, sports car, motorbike they always promised themselves. Those art lessons, that photographic equipment, that diving gear . . .

And they stop doing things they hate. *Life's too short* they tell themselves, knowing that, in their case, it truly could be. They learn to say no to people who want their time. They become more, or less, ambitious. More, or less, focused. They might change jobs. They prioritize.

Nick, maybe, is taking his mid-life crisis early. That's what the cancer has done for him: pulled it forward in time. For what is a mid-life crisis, but a forced appreciation that one day you will die, and that there is no going back? That you have left behind you the longest, sweetest, most exciting period of your life and that in front of you, along with all the good things still to come, are the inevitable nasties. The death of your parents, if they haven't already died, the gradual – or not so gradual – failure of your body. The loss of your looks, your strength. The loss of your friends. Illness or disability. Your death.

But, usually, you have years to accommodate yourself to these. It's only when you have a life-threatening disease, like cancer, that the facts of death are thrust in your face, all at once.

In the six weeks since Nick was interviewed by the Sunday paper he has been a guest on three radio programmes. He has contributed an album choice column for a Saturday newspaper supplement and been featured and photographed again – this time in the cottage – for a *Day in the Life* article in a glossy mag. I didn't recognize the living room in the photo, with the furniture reorganized and instruments artfully scattered around. It looked like a pretentious guitar grotto to me. Nick doesn't seem to mind being ludicrously represented. His attitude seems to be the more fantastic, the more unrelated to his real life, the better. He has two more interviews lined up, one with a tabloid newspaper, one with a music magazine. He has also been approached by a London publisher with the suggestion that he writes a book, content unspecified, except not fiction. And not *How to Learn Guitar* either, I suspect. *Groupies I Have Known* or *My Life on the Rock Track* sound more likely titles. Nick is undecided. He says he'll have a think and get back to them. He has told them that his high-profile rock period was short, compared to others, and neither excessive (sex or drugwise) or especially newsworthy. However they say they have a hunch about him; that if he 'put himself about' he could be really 'hot'.

I have pointed out to Nick that 'putting himself about', at least physically, is exactly what he used to hate. But he says that he holds the power now. He doesn't need them. He has no one pressurizing him with a finger on the small print of a contract, telling him what to do, when, and where. These days, emissaries of the big wide world can come to him, he doesn't have to go to them. He can set his own rules and have them accepted as life-style choices, not as symptoms of disability, because he set it up that way in the first interview.

He has told me that there is no masterplan and I believe him. He is, nonetheless, considering changes to his life. He is open to them. And if he is open to them, this is acknowledgement that there might be more to his future than living here in his little house in his little provincial town, working in his small-town shop, and playing with his small-town groups. Partnered by his unfashionable, small-town girlfriend. I see him as having been on a long quiet journey away from the mainland and finding himself suddenly, after that first interview, within sight of harbour lights again. During his long quiet journey he acquired a partner, me. Now, I wonder about my status. Am I – have I been – his ship-mate, who has made the journey easier and more enjoyable, but whose company will be shed on dry land? Or am I the native princess he has wooed and won in the wildlands, and will bring home in triumph on his arm?

Perhaps he just wants change – any change – in his life. Who can blame him? He can't change his actual life, but he can change the trappings. He can make a symbolic move. Perhaps the direction he is drifting in is entirely fortuitous. A hand was offered to him, reaching out to him from his past, and because he wants and needs change, and can see no reason not to take it, he is taking it.

I am busier at work than ever. In a few weeks the petition forms have to be presented to the Prime Minister, so they're pouring, no, thumping in. Francine has already taken one car-load up to London to store at her flat, and another goes up next weekend. The petition will be one of the events of a Forest Action Day at Westminster, and the organizers have promised to provide us with a decorated trolley, when the Day comes, at least the size of a British Rail trolley, plus enough muscle power to pull it. All we have to do is deliver the goods to No. 10, and prepare a speech for any attendant media. The presentation is scheduled for 11.00 a.m. – the afternoon is reserved for lobbying MPs and speeches in the Palace of Westminster's Grand Committee Room – so I'll have to go up with Francine in her car the night before and stay over with her at the flat. As it's only a two-bedroomed apartment she has notified our plans to Lionel, who occasionally stays there himself midweek, to ensure that our occupancies won't clash. She wrote to him rather than using the phone, because she can't trust herself at the moment not to be rude to him. Her solicitor has been complaining bitterly about his behaviour. He called the poor woman a bitch the other day – over the phone –

because she did indeed ask for, and get, a restraining order to keep his assets in this country. Francine is enraged by his bullying attitude but at the same time terrified that if she becomes abusive herself he will retaliate with one of the trump cards he undoubtedly holds, and do something drastic like withholding Philip's school fees.

Today, Francine and a balding man called Charles who is Francine's accountant are poring over documents in her kitchen, and must not be disturbed till lunchtime. The exclusion order applies to Celia too, who is flitting hither and thither through the rest of the house, including my office, like a neurotic moth. Either she is having a mental breakdown or she wants something. When she comes in for the third time and hovers behind me, making a Tinkerbellish noise with her bracelets, I put my pen down and say, 'Celia. Can I help?'

'Oh, no,' she says immediately. But then moves further into the room, diffidently, and says, 'Well . . . actually . . .'

I push my chair back and look willing. Celia has grown the nails on her right hand very long. To pluck at her guitar with, I assume. She touches her lower lip with the long thumb nail. 'There was something I wanted to ask . . .'

'Fire away.'

She edges her small bottom on to one of my piles

of boxes. 'D'you think,' she says, 'that . . . um . . .' – she frowns down at her loop pile sweater and plucks at it – 'that . . . that Jason is trustworthy?'

Good heavens. What is she suggesting? Is she questioning Jason's honesty?

She looks up, sees my face, and continues in a rush. 'About what he says. Sorry. Sorry.' She smiles. 'Trustworthy's the wrong word . . . I mean . . . *right*. About Nick.'

About Nick? 'What does Jason say about Nick?'

Celia flutters her hands. 'That, you know, with all the stuff in the papers . . . and on the radio . . . that Nick might start a new group.'

'Jason said that Nick is going to start a new group?'

'Well, or something, you know . . . only, well . . .' She takes a breath, and suddenly plunges in. Her expression radiates enthusiasm. 'It's really exciting, isn't it? He could be famous again. I mean' – her blue eyes are wide and thrilled – 'We could know someone famous . . .'

I feel unpleasantly prised away from Nick. That 'we' undermines my confidence, since I hear it as including me, and seems to suggest that our relationships with Nick are comparable.

'Jason's terrifically excited,' Celia says. She nods to reinforce this, but then pulls a small face and adds, as if it's an unimportant afterthought, 'Though obviously he's a bit worried about the shop. Nick hasn't said anything, but . . .'

'The shop?'

'Yes. You know . . . he might sell it, if he gets involved in other things . . .'

'Whatever happens, I can't see Nick wanting to sell the shop. He's not joining or starting another professional band. I've heard no suggestion of that. Other things might happen, I suppose. But if anything Jason should get more responsibility, not less.'

'Oh, well, that's good.' But Celia says it carelessly, as if this is a side issue. She leans forward and fixes me with a warm, encouraging gaze. 'You must be excited too, though, with all this. You must be.'

'That's one way of describing it.' I refuse to be drawn into confidences regarding Nick. I imagine Celia round at the shop, gossiping with Jason. Speculating about Nick, his dramas, his future. She seems to want me to join in. To say, *Oh my God, yes, it's so exciting, and you'll never guess what's happening next* . . . A response that allies me to her and Jason, as fans of Nick's life. Or is she testing the ground over something? Or testing me? Why the hell is she at the shop all the time? How can Jason and Nick be so tolerant? Hasn't she got any friends of her own?

Bluntly I ask, 'Are you going back to university in September?'

Celia hesitates, then pulls back and says, 'I expect so.' She gets down from the boxes. She knows she has been rebuffed, but seems unbothered. In fact she looks mildly pleased with herself, in an obscure, mission-accomplished way. She flashes me a smile. 'Well. You can tell Nick I'm excited for him, anyway.'

'Why not tell him yourself.' I suppress the words *you impudent child* and substitute, in case I've sounded rude, 'I'm sure he'd be touched.'

She murmurs, 'Well, yes, I suppose I might,' and floats to the door. A little wave back to me, and she's gone. I scowl down at my work. What the hell was all that about? She's muddled me. She sounds so innocent, and yet everything she says stirs me up. Attacks my security. When she came in she said she wanted to ask me something, but I can recollect no real question. She just rhapsodized about Nick, and tried to get me to do the same. Perhaps she really was testing me. Finding out where I stand. Whether I'm encouraging him or not. Whether I'm his supporter, or whether there's a vacancy . . .

This is paranoia. I distract myself by recalling what she said about Jason and the shop. He has no reason for anxiety, I'm sure, but a reassurance wouldn't hurt. Perhaps his security feels shaky too. Maybe we are all picking up Nick's indecision and restlessness. All waiting to see which way he's going to jump. It's as if we've all accepted that he's got to jump somewhere.

I end the day weary. I have done nothing physical – no boxes to be lugged around today – and yet my shoulders ache as if I have been loading a lorry. I drive back to my flat and slump into the armchair for twenty minutes. But then my legs start to ache too – almost a menstrual ache, except I'm not due. I know the cure. Eventually I heave myself up, change into tracksuit and running shoes, and leave the building. I'll go to the park this evening, and then the river.

The effort of running is massive at first. My limbs are heavy, dead lumps of meat. They have no life, no tone, no energy. It takes a while to achieve any sort of rhythm. I imagine my legs as dough. I've watched Francine make wholemeal bread: transforming the leaden, solid, grey-brown mixture with her kneading, her thumping, into a rubbery sponge-like substance that springs back when she pushes at it. Suddenly organic and alive. That is what happens to your flesh, eventually, when you run. You push the blood round. You force your muscles to be exercised, oxygenated, into life. Then, suddenly, you reach the crossover point; your brain can switch off, and your body takes over.

But entering the park I am still focused outwards, conscious of my surroundings, still pushing myself. The park is flat and municipally dull but nonetheless well-used; the bandstand at its centre is a popular young people's meeting place. There are complaints now and then about the litter they scatter around the concrete, even that their very presence is intimidating to other park users. But what's a bandstand for, in the middle of a public park, if not for friends to meet under? When I was a teenager we used a bus shelter. People tried to banish us from that, too . . .

This is how it goes. You move from attending to your body, to seeing what is around you, and then turn back in on yourself. There is progression to your thoughts as you run, but no great logic. Attempting to order thoughts when running is akin to building a tower of bricks on a trampoline. But bouncing thoughts can be new, surprising, refreshed thoughts.

I leave the park and the bandstand behind and cross the road to the river meadows. I have some sort of revelation when I reach the river bridge. No, not a revelation, more a sudden confirmation. I stop a moment to gaze over the stone parapet at the town weir. There are two evening fishermen in waders just above the fall, their lines in the deep water below. The confirmation that comes to me is that I am right in the feelings I have been experiencing with regard to Nick: that I am being left behind. That I cannot make the break from his illness. Others have done it. Nick is moving on from it, or trying to. Our friends and acquaintances see the crisis as over. My mother has done so since before Christmas. Everyone is looking beyond his cancer, pushing it away, moving on.

But the crux of the confirmation is not just that I am indeed having these left-behind feelings – obviously I am – but that I am right to have them. Because it isn't over, is it? It's only eleven months since his operation. If it were all over, why does the hospital still insist on seeing him every three months? Why do they draw his blood and examine it through microscopes? Why do they X-ray his lungs? Why do they make him undress and scrutinize his body? Why would they do this, if they thought he was cured?

Or am I truly the party-pooper? Are these checks merely routine? An automatic procedure, however tiny the risk? Everyone with cancer is followed up and checked out. Even if the doctors know they're cured. Perhaps I'm simply too tired to move on. I am depressed still, I know. It's understandable, surely. No one will draw a line under this illness for us, so I can't either. No, more than that, I *will not* draw a line. Someone has to remember the gods. They must be given no excuse for revenge. Until the line is drawn, someone has to carry the fear standard. My one ally, I suddenly sense, was Toby. He understood. But he's dead.

I turn away from the bridge. I realize I'm hungry. What I fancy, right now, is a gourmet lasagne from Nick's freezer.

I run along the river bank. The cinder path has become busy – there are people, bounding dogs, children, everywhere. Their voices are loud but somehow snatched and lost in the waterside air. I leave the path and cut across the dry meadow. I can half circle the town out here; by the time I rejoin the streets I will be less than ten minutes from Nick's cottage. I hadn't planned to see him this evening, but that's definitely where I'm going.

As I jog up the lane I actually see him from a distance; he's standing outside the cottage, on the flagstone hardstanding of the small front garden, staring up at the white-rendered frontage. As I draw close he turns; he looks surprised and pleased to see me. He has a beautiful smile and it comes to me, with as much pain as pleasure, that I couldn't bear to be without it.

'A problem?' I ask, slowing to a walk. He is wearing the grey denim shirt I bought him for Christmas, open over a black T-shirt. I am stupidly moved; he wears my favours, even when he doesn't expect to see me.

He gazes back at the cottage. 'Grubby, isn't it? How much masonry paint d'you reckon I'd need?'

I turn to examine the frontage. He's right; there are grey mould streaks on the right of the building, the side more shaded by the hedge trees. And green algae stains below the downstairs window sills.

'There must be a rule of thumb,' I say. 'The shop'd know.' Why is Nick thinking about painting his cottage? Because he's definitely staying? Because he's definitely going? Or just because it is May, and the cottage needs painting?

'Celia was asking about you at work,' I say.

'Really?' Nick stops scrutinizing the wall. 'What about me?'

'She seemed to think you might be going back into

the business. Playing professionally. Starting, or joining, another band.'

Nick stares at me. 'What gave her that idea?'

'Jason, I believe. Presumably you gave the idea to him. All this attention you've been getting.'

Nick turns away. He looks overcome. Why won't he deny it? Just say, *stupid kids, I'm not planning anything*. I can't decide if the gnawing sensation inside me really is hunger, or something more unpleasant.

After a moment he clears his throat. 'I haven't decided anything,' he says. 'I haven't even decided if I need to decide anything.'

This isn't at all what I want to hear. I want him to be dismissive. To sweep other people's speculations aside. I am so unfair. Why, when I'm so muddled myself – and that's what it is, that's my problem with Celia, I know it is – can't I allow him to be confused too?

And yet I can't. I hate it. I know that in my own tiredness, muddle and insecurity the qualities I want from a partner at the moment are certainty, energy and clear thinking. I want a rock; someone to lean on. I'm tired, desperately tired, of propping myself up.

A sickening thought comes to me: that although I do love Nick, and care about him, that, right now, I need someone else. Someone unproblematic.

'Are you hungry?' he asks.

I nod. I will pretend that the gnawing is hunger. I can always eat.

We go inside and he zaps a lasagne for me in the microwave. He's already eaten. I watch him moving around the kitchen. It's an ordinary evening. He looks very ordinary now. An ordinary youngish man, relaxed and domestically occupied in his own kitchen. He has no limp. He is not thin. The physical signs are hidden: the two long white scars, one on his thigh, one above his groin. Outwardly, this scene could be happening a year ago. Except that it isn't, and everything has changed.

We need someone to tell us that the cancer is gone, the ordeal over. As long as they can't, or won't, the ordeal can't be over. A human being can only take so much. Then they need a rest. And a change, they say, is as good as a rest.

After I've eaten, I decide that I am being doubly unfair if I don't give Nick the chance to be strong and unproblematic. He knows me well, but he can't read my mind. I push my plate away.

'Celia upset me,' I say. 'She made me feel that she knows things about you that I don't.'

Nick is sitting opposite me. He has been watching me eat.

'You know she's wrong.'

'I'm very easily upset at the moment,' I admit. 'I feel unsettled.'

'Yes.' Nick smiles thinly. 'It's in the air.'

I note his smile. 'That's the wrong answer.'

'Sorry.'

'Is there anything I should know?'

'About what?'

'You. Us.'

He hesitates. 'Us. I don't think so. Me. I don't know.'

'Oh God.' I sigh.

He pulls back. Looks away to the window. He thinks I want him to be honest, and he's doing his best.

I say, 'I hate this. I'm sorry. I think I'm frightened.'

Nick looks back at me. 'You don't have to be frightened. I promise. Whatever happens.'

'That's easy to say.'

'Who else would have me, now I'm covered in scars?'

He's trying to be flippant. It's a way of smothering anxiety. He must know that one way to detach yourself from someone is to imagine that someone detaching his or herself from you. It works both ways, once it's started, back and forth, in a to and fro of panic. After a while it's impossible to say where the break started.

He says, quietly, 'I need you.'

I correct him. 'You needed me.'

'No.' He shakes his head. 'I don't mean that. Gratitude has nothing to do with it.'

'Scars on men can be sexy,' I say. It's true. The stigmata of a macho life.

'Not cancer scars,' he says.

'I want it all to be over,' I say. 'I've had enough.'

His face freezes. I suddenly realize he has misunderstood me. 'The cancer,' I say quickly. 'I mean the cancer.' But I saw him, just for a moment, as a man believing I wanted to leave him. The look on his face should have reassured me, but it doesn't. Another revelation. It is his attachment to me that is insupportable. His weight. I want him to love me and need me and not leave me, at the same time as his love and neediness and disinclination to leave exhausts me. He cannot win.

I admit it. 'I am impossible. I'm sorry. I'm so confused.'

'You're tired,' he says. 'We're both tired.'

'Yes.'

And that's it. We let the subject go. Tiredness isn't the answer – or not the whole answer, anyway – but it will do for the moment. You can't tackle what hasn't ended. You can't accommodate to an unknown.

Nick behaves for the rest of the evening like a man who knows he has disappointed in some way and wants to atone for it. He washes up my supper things, makes us both a coffee, settles me on the sofa in the living room and sits down close beside me. After the coffee, while we're watching some half-funny sit-com on the television, he draws my head first against his chest, and then on to his lap.

'You should get yourself another cat,' I say, as he strokes my head. It's meant to be therapeutic, isn't it, stroking a pet.

He flicks my ear. 'I'm thinking about it.'

Cats don't like travel. They like being in one place, with their stay-at-home doting master. He's thinking about it. Stroking is good for the pet too. I begin to relax. We have acknowledged something this evening. Confession, as they say, is good for the soul. Our problems are not solved or even diminished by acknowledging they exist, but exposing them is a relief.

I see the start of the nine o'clock news, but can't make sense of anything, partly because, lying like this, the picture is incomprehensible. And the sound is too low for me to hear with one ear. I drift off. The next thing I know the green VCR clock, which is directly in my line of vision, says three-thirty.

'Nick?' I whisper. I'm appallingly cold.

'Uh-huh?' His voice above me sounds distant.

'Wake up.'

'I am.'

I lift my head from his thighs. With difficulty. I have been lying awkwardly; the muscles of my neck and shoulder have locked. 'For God's sake. Why didn't you wake me?'

'I didn't like to. You seemed to need it.'

I rub at my shoulder and shiver. He pushes me up properly and switches off the table lamp. We creak to our feet like old people and start to organize ourselves for bed. Letting me sleep on him was a touching idea, but it's left me bone-achingly cold. I feel thin and frail as I totter up the stairs, as if I have been unpeeled, and in bed I take a long time to warm up, even folded in Nick's arms.

And lying there I keep seeing a picture of the two of us downstairs, and I wonder what Nick found to think about, sitting on his own for all that time, with my sleeping head in his lap.

Chapter 8

It is unfortunately the case that affliction with one woe does not protect you against attack by others. Rather the contrary. Weakened or distracted by a first calamity, you fall easy prey to a second. You lose your job, say, don't bother to get the boiler serviced because that would be a hundred quid you can't afford and the thing is running fine, and next thing you know you've gassed your family with fumes and no amount of money will bring them back. Or, little Jimmy is desperately ill, and you're so anxious and involved in visiting him in hospital that you neglect your other offspring and they become criminally delinquent to show that they need your attention too . . .

Or . . . well, these are just cheerful examples. And I'm thinking here, actually, not of Nick or myself, but of Francine. It is the last Tuesday in June and yesterday she broke her leg in a car crash, an accident that appears to have been entirely her own fault. She is a spirited driver normally; divorce stress seems to have exacerbated 'spirited' into 'reckless'. The accident happened less than a mile from her house, the town end of the lane. At its start this lane is in effect single track, because few of the estate houses there have garages and the residents line the kerb with cars. (Francine's countrified end is much more moneyed and well provided-for, of course; many houses are triple garaged.) Francine knows, as everyone who uses the lane does, that driving out from town it is prudent to swing cautiously off the main road, in case a car in the lane is approaching the junction. But on this occasion she wasn't remotely cautious – according to the driver of the sludge tanker she smacked into, at any rate. The road surface was dry, the noon light unsunny but excellent; to buckle the front of her Citroën as impressively as she apparently has, one of the vehicles must have been travelling at speed. This is much more likely to have been Francine, swinging up into her home straight, than the tanker driver almost on top of a give-way junction. I have noticed that Francine is permanently in a hurry these days; stress definitely afflicts her with time-deprivation symptoms. And because she was alone in the car she had no one to shout *slow down* at her – I expect she was mentally months away, in a divorce courtroom, probably. I'm just glad it was a large vehicle she met – the tanker driver was unscathed, the impact happening feet below his cab – and not one of the other lane residents, or me.

She is quite seriously injured. She has broken her right tibia and fibula and her big toe on the same leg. Her thigh is badly bruised. Which is stronger, a steering wheel or a thigh bone? Well, the steering wheel is bent into a half moon, according to Celia, while her mother's thigh bone, though the flesh around it is hugely swollen with bruising, is intact.

I was at work at the time, and, thinking back, Celia and I may have actually heard the sirens of the emergency vehicles attending the crash, though we thought nothing of them. It wasn't until Celia poked her head into my office at nearly 1.30 and said, 'Is Mum here? She said she'd be back for lunch,' that I even grasped that Francine was not in the house.

And it was at that moment, with Celia's body still tilted through my doorway, that the house phone in the kitchen rang. Celia left the door open and went to answer it. I knew, the moment I heard the distant cadences of her voice, without being able to distinguish a word of what she was saying, that something was wrong. Shock seems to stiffen, even solidify, the air around its victims, and the atmospheric change is detectable a great distance away.

I rose immediately and went to the kitchen. Celia was nodding into the telephone receiver. The changes in her face were frightening; I could see her flesh bleach as blood drained from her cheeks. I expect the same effect was visible in my face a year ago, as I sat in my office listening to Nick telling me he had cancer.

I guessed she was speaking to someone official. Police, or hospital staff. It sounded like a male voice. She finished nodding into the receiver, said, 'Yes, right now,' and put it down. She turned to me. 'Mum's had a car accident. She's hurt her legs.' She looked around as if she had lost something. 'I must . . . I must . . .'

'I'll take you,' I said. Celia drives, but doesn't have her own car. She'd have to take a taxi, otherwise, or ask a neighbour for a lift.

It's only a twelve-minute drive to the hospital. Francine had been taken to the General, on the northern outskirts of town. Nick had had his first out-patient appointment there, before referral to the teaching hospital, but I hadn't gone with him. I was last at the General five years ago, visiting Grace on the gynae ward when she had her endometriosis diagnosed. Celia sat stiff and correct beside me in the Golf and half-way there said that the hospital had told her to go to Accident and Emergency, because Francine was still there, waiting to go into theatre. I said, 'Right,' and, 'I'm sure she's fine, Celia, you mustn't worry,' and not much else, at that point; I had a feeling that hospitals never told you very bad news over the phone, and I was bracing myself for discovering that Francine was fatally injured. Even dead.

But I was wrong. The A and E department of the glass and concrete hospital is compact, inside its box-like sixties lobby, and as we introduced ourselves to the receptionist I could actually hear Francine's voice, coming from a curtained-off cubicle in the treatment area behind the desk. The voice sounded tired but relievingly strong, and was saying, 'Not even a glass of water? Oh dear.'

We were taken straight to her. She was more than simply alive and capable of speech. She was pale and the pupils of her eyes were tiny, making the blue irises huge, but she was half sitting up on the trolley-bed and fully conscious. A moment ago, hearing her voice outside, I'd felt the urge to run to her and hug her. But now, seeing her, the impulse died. She'd have been embarrassed, and pushed me off.

'Oh good,' she said as she saw us. 'Celia, darling.' She reached out and drew her daughter to her side. 'I'm so sorry, dear. You must have been terrified when they rang. And Jess. Thank goodness you were there.'

Celia said breathily, 'Mummy, they said they were going to operate. What are they going to do?'

'Set the leg, I suppose,' Francine said. 'You mustn't worry. Everything's under control. And everyone is charming. They've done hundreds of X-rays. I've broken the two lower bones. Just on this side. And my poor big toe. Oh dear.' The effort of speaking seemed to overwhelm her. She tipped her head back into the pillow and closed her eyes. Then opened them again. 'Don't ask me anything else, dear, there's a good girl. They've injected me with painkillers. It's really quite interesting. Do I sound sensible?'

We assured her that she did. In fact she sounded

not only sensible, but over-politely so. How drunks sound sometimes, picking their way around normal. I suspected that her real self was so heavily sedated that only the automatic shell of good manners was functioning. As it always would be. In people like Francine, the show always goes on.

That was yesterday. Today Francine is still in hospital, and will remain there until the consultant decides that her bruising has subsided enough for her and her plastered leg to get around safely and comfortably on crutches. Probably at least till Thursday.

Some of the ramifications of Francine's disablement have had to be faced today. The number of people one accident can affect; Celia spent most of yesterday evening and this morning on the telephone. She's rung her father, her grandmother, her brother – or rather, his school housemaster – the cleaning lady (who is normally collected by car) and all those friends of her mother's whose imminent gatherings Francine now won't be attending. Just this week there were two dinner engagements and one theatre trip.

Our work plans too are going to be seriously affected. It has occurred to me that Francine is most unlikely to want – or be able – to go to London with me in nine days (the Thursday of next week) to deliver the forest petitions. There are two car/taxi loads to be physically transferred from the Embankment flat to

Westminster. Even if she were well enough otherwise – which is doubtful – this is not a job for a woman on crutches. The realization that I will have to tackle the job alone sinks into me like an unwelcome but immovable weight. There is no escape. The petitions have to be delivered, and on that day. Someone has to take responsibility, and that someone, clearly, given the circumstances, has to be me. I must leave nothing to Francine.

I do mention to Celia that there will have to be a change in the petition presentation plans, but warn her not to say anything to Francine yet. 'If she raises the subject herself,' I tell her, 'say we've thought about it and it's all sorted. She mustn't worry.'

Celia nods with efficient understanding. She has recovered from the shock she was in yesterday afternoon and now, in sole charge of the house and its contents and equipment, has transmogrified into an astonishingly effective young woman. Despite my prejudice against her, I am impressed. She knows how to operate all the domestic machinery, from dishwasher to fax machine. She knows how to sort the post: what to open, and what to pass on to me. She was already up, watering the tubs that stand on the terrace overlooking the vast back garden, when I arrived at eight-thirty this morning. For a moment I thought she was Francine; even her bearing seems more adult. She has made meals for herself over twenty-four hours now and the kitchen has not degenerated into a slum. In fact

I actually asked if she had eaten anything since the accident, because the table and work surfaces looked so pristine. She assured me she had. 'There's masses in the freezer,' she said airily. 'I just helped myself.' And to think that last night I'd been so anxious about her that I'd checked that she was prepared to stay in the house alone. I was going to suggest she invite a girl-friend in. Or, at a pinch, I might have offered myself. Luckily she said she'd be fine.

This afternoon I have finished everything I need to do in the office and the time is close to four, when hospital visiting hours officially start. (Celia visited this morning, but only close relatives are tolerated out of hours.) I am off to visit Francine as a friend, but also to get her signature on two urgent cheques.

The layout of the in-patient block of the General is very different to Nick's hospital, but the building smells the same. A white, institutional bathroom smell: stiff laundered towels with a trace of mouthwash. The flattening shadowless light is the same too. And the lifts; Francine's ward is on the fourth floor and I have to operate one of the familiar stainless steel contraptions. They are Schindler's lifts. I remember how, in Nick's hospital, I used to stare at that name, engraved in the steel to the right of the control panel, as I ascended to his floor. Schindler was a German who saved Jews in the war. Not this Schindler, presumably.

This one shuts you in a shiny metal box and whizzes you up and down, quietly and efficiently, through a place of healing. Perhaps it could be the same one.

Leaving the lift I follow the arrows along a wide corridor with no natural lighting. There is a flicker in the artificial lights that illuminate the suspended ceiling. I am feeling disoriented already; the flicker sets off a small palpitation in my chest. A couple of staff dressed entirely in white pass by, their rubber-soled shoes squeaking on the polished floor. I tell myself I have not really entered a surreal sci-fi film, and nor was the lift a time machine, transporting me back a year. This is all quite different.

Entering the ward the uncomfortable reminders are forgotten. I read from the chalk board opposite the reception desk that Francine is in Room C. Room C is further down the corridor. A maroon-uniformed woman is wheeling a tea trolley ahead of me. It makes a wonderfully reassuring clanking, clinking sound, like tea trolleys the world over.

I turn into Room C. There are six beds, three patients present. Francine is one of them. She is lying on her bed, not in it, wearing a soft white tie-wrap dressing gown. Her eyes are closed. But she's not asleep. As I approach the bed her lids lift.

She smiles, almost lazily. 'Hello, Jess. Celia said you were coming.' She looks down at herself, spreading a hand over her lower body. It's a gesture of regret, apology. 'Idiot, aren't I?'

'You said it.' I sit down carefully on the striped cover at the foot of the bed. The top of her locker and the adjacent wide shelf that runs to the room wash hand-basin are a mass of flowers. All hers; the other patients have smaller spreads on and around their own lockers. Francine's friends must work fast. The tallest blooms are a bunch of white lilies, the flower heads still tightly furled. There is something voluptuously fleshy, almost genital, about furled lily heads.

Francine sees my gaze and laughs. 'From Lionel, of course. Preposterous, aren't they? And he knows I loathe cut flowers. Still, they impress the nurses.'

I didn't know Francine disliked cut flowers. I think of her house as flower-filled; but they're on plants, of course, alive in their pots. I'm glad I didn't think to stop at the flower kiosk. It's only just occurred to me, looking at this display, that most people do take gifts of some sort to the sick. I haven't brought anything. I never took anything to Nick either, I realize, except items he specifically asked for. (And sometimes, as with the sawn-off shot gun, not even those.) I must have subconsciously assumed – as perhaps I'm doing now – that presenting myself was enough.

'How's the leg?' The plaster is brilliant white and encases her right leg from toe to knee. The surface is as yet unmarked. I don't suppose she'll allow anyone to scribble on it. The two inches of thigh flesh above, all I can see below the dressing gown, are tinged purple.

'Nightmare,' Francine sighs. 'I don't want to think about it. The doctor says I won't be driving for weeks.'

I'd meant, does it hurt?, but she's just thinking of practicalities. Pain, presumably, is not at the forefront of her mind. Francine loves driving, which is fortunate, since she has to do a lot of it. She won't be put off by an accident.

'I'm sure Celia will run you around,' I assure her. 'She's being terribly efficient. She's arranged for your garage to give you a courtesy car already.'

'Oh yes?' Francine's eyes narrow. 'What is it?'

I smile. 'Nothing flash. A diesel Peugeot, I believe. Red.'

Francine sniffs her approval. Her complexion is very pale, I realize – it's the white gown that initially fools you. Her extremities – hands, unplastered foot, even nose – look fragile. Delicate and vulnerable. Her hands are deeply scored with age lines. I never noticed before.

'They have a portable pay phone here,' she says. 'Very clever. It's on wheels.'

'Yes,' I say. 'I think they're common in hospitals. They had them in Nick's too.'

'I've rung Lionel's secretary and told him he'll have to collect Philip from school at the weekend. He's got far too much luggage for the train and I'm not sending Celia. She's never driven there before. She'd get hopelessly lost.'

'He's home next week, is he?' I'm always surprised

by how short public school terms are. Hardly value for money. The town comprehensive won't break up till late July. My mind turns over possibilities. If Philip is home he could keep an eye on Francine, and perhaps Celia could come up to London with me. She knows the flat . . .

'Only for the weekend,' says Francine. 'Then he's off to the Dordogne for three weeks with a school friend.'

Oh well. I jettison that plan. I'm spared six hours in a car with Celia, anyway. And sharing an evening in a small flat with her. Though I do wonder when Francine ever gets to know her son. He's always either away at school, or off with friends. Last summer it was Canada for six weeks.

I remember the cheques then, and pull them out of my work folder. Francine reaches for a pen. It may be only twenty-four hours since she surfaced from a general anaesthetic, but she still wants an update on the work they relate to.

'And now listen,' she says afterwards, putting the pen aside. 'About this petition presentation. I can't see myself being able to go to London with you.'

'I know.' I nod quickly, to give the impression that this is not a big issue, that solutions are ten-a-penny. 'It's all right. I'll deal with it.'

'Yes.' This is obviously what Francine has in mind anyway. Being superwoman herself, she attributes the same virtuoso powers to others. 'I'm sure you'll manage. I'll give you the flat keys. You'll have to take a car, because there'll be a couple more boxes of forms to take with you, and they'll be impossible on a train. But if you don't want to take yours, we'll hire one. The flat's easy to find and it's got its own car park in the basement – it couldn't be more convenient, honestly. Really the only problem will be getting the boxes from the flat to Westminster. You'll use taxis, obviously, but they'll still have to be loaded. That would be much easier with two. Why don't you take Nick?'

This solution has not occurred to me. Nick hates travel. He especially hates motorway travel. There is no way from here to London – unless you want to spend all day driving – that doesn't involve the M4.

'That's impossible, is it?' Francine says.

'Um. Not necessarily. I just hadn't thought of him.'

'He might be useful at the presentation,' Francine says. 'Celia tells me he's going to be famous again. The television people will be there. We could introduce him.'

I smile thinly. That's it, I think; pile on the pressure. This is what will always happen, whenever he sticks his head over a parapet. 'I'll ask him,' I say. 'But don't count on it.'

I have to leave a couple of minutes later, because two of Francine's friends turn up. They are women in their forties, exquisitely dressed in summer suits and bearing baskets of luscious, colourfully arranged fruit. As she greets them Francine's voice becomes louder and more ringing, to match theirs. I'd love to stay, because I adore the way Francine and her friends are so relentlessly and cheerfully rude to each other, but I know it's not my place. They are always boringly pleasant to me; I'm the employee, not one of them.

I see Nick that evening at my flat after supper. We don't always meet at his cottage any more; these days we're as likely to be here as there. It must have occurred to Nick, as well as to me, that I was always – usually literally – making the running. He arrives at the flat at eight, and the first thing he does is rush to the kitchen and hold his hand under the cold water tap, because he's been to see a friend whose cat has kittens, and while he was inspecting them the mother bit him below the knuckle of his thumb. He's still bleeding profusely.

'Did you choose one?' I ask.

'Yup.' He sucks at the side of his hand. 'Ah God. Ferocious animal. A tabby female. Blue eyes. Revoltingly cute. Be ready in a week or so. How's Francine?'

'Remarkable. She may have smashed her leg in three places but she has an intact backbone.' I smile. It is one of Francine's most dismissive expressions of contempt, that an individual, occupational group, nationality, whatever, lacks backbone. 'She'll be out of action for a while though. And . . .' Is this a good moment, while he's half distracted with cat-bite wounds? 'She won't be able to make the presentation emotions. Why can't I love this man *and* be happy about it?

'I want you to come with me to London,' I say. 'But I don't need you. I could manage on my own. I'd just prefer not to.'

Nick frowns, says he understands, and promises to think about it. We leave it that if he comes – which he well might, he says – he will be doing it just for me. There will be no question of media attention for him. And even so, he needs a few days to get used to the idea.

Chapter 9

We are the victims, I think, of either a conspiracy, or a very sick joke. Possibly a conspiratorial sick joke. We set it up, didn't we, with the suggestion of that trip to London. We were caught out, counting next week's chickens, taking fate for granted. I should have known. I should have kept my guard up. I am so angry.

Nick has his excuse not to go to London. It is an excellent excuse. Unarguable with.

During examination at his Monday outpatient appointment he – or the consultant, I'm not sure which – noticed another lump. Not on his shin this time – that lump has dissipated completely – but on his forearm. It is at the side of the upper muscle sheaf, about half-way between wrist and elbow. The skin can be moved freely over it, so, whatever it is, it is attached to the muscle below.

Nick says the consultant was at first dismissive, but

through to me this time. It's tried whispering: *you can save him; all that reorganization for nothing, it's irresistible*, but I'm not listening. I've had enough of hospitals and fear and hope and loneliness and not talking about any of this. Nick would run away too, if he could. It's not my fault that he's physically attached to the enemy.

I've told him that I'll come back from London as quickly as I can. I've said I won't stay after the presentation and I'll return straight to his cottage. I might manage it by four; he won't even be back from the hospital by then. So, I've said to him, I will know the news almost as soon as he does. I will be there for him when he gets home.

The words were easy to say. Though even as I said them, I wasn't absolutely sure I meant them.

Last time we told Jason but no one else. This time we haven't told anyone. No one would thank us. This way we keep the damage small and self-contained. If it detonates into disaster, people will know soon enough. My mother rang earlier today and said I sounded very tense. I blamed the preparations for London. Silly of me – it gave her ideas. 'London? When are you driving back, dear?' she cried. 'You must call in.' My mother's house is only ten miles from the motorway at Reading.

'I don't think I can,' I said. But I couldn't think of any credible reason to back this, except the real one. I said – and I thought I was lying, I swear it – that there was a possibility I might not go straight home. That there might be other things to do. Other events I ought to attend. Sorry, Mum, I said, but . . . but . . . don't nag, Mum . . .

My mother can recognize a tizz when she hears one. An overloaded refusal to take decisions. She sighed and said, 'It's all right, Jessica. Don't worry. It was just a suggestion. If you can't manage it you can't. If you can, I'd love to see you.'

She put the phone down without asking after Nick. People have stopped doing that. Half the world doesn't ask because it doesn't know there's anything to ask about, and the other half, which includes myself, doesn't want to know. Poor Nick.

It's Wednesday evening now, and I've stayed with Nick right up to my departure this afternoon. Having made up my mind to desert him for the important moment I've found myself more tolerant of his fear, and more able to give him reassurance. Guilt, I suppose. Tonight, to avoid being alone, he is playing a gig; even if I'd been here I'd have encouraged him to do this, and probably gone along too. The gig is at the Foundry, which is an old-fashioned rock/blues pub, and he's playing with the resident band while their lead guitarist is in Scotland wetting the head of his first grandchild. Yes, genuine dinosaurs; Nick will be the youngest player by at least ten years. But the punters – who range from bearded headmasters to bikers – think they're brilliant and by the end of the evening all they'll want to hear are old classics like 'Walking' and 'I've Got the Blues for You' played à la Gary Moore, whose sound Nick can reproduce on his old Gibson – his most valuable electric guitar – down to the last mournful note-bend. As long as he doesn't let the sentimentality of the music overwhelm him he'll have a good, mind-occupying evening.

It's 7.00 p.m. now and my journey to London is nearly over. I am approaching my childhood territory. I was born in Richmond. London is like an ancient branch of the family I don't see very often and vaguely disapprove of, but nevertheless have to acknowledge a connection with. Something not unpleasant happens inside me as I approach it. I recognize an emotional bond. But it is an ambivalent bond. Proximity to Londoners makes me feel – depending on who they are, and my mood at the time – either a clod-hopping hick, or vastly superior. A clod-hopping hick because Londoners are so busy and fast and wear peculiar clothes that look dowdy and dated but turn out to be fashionable, and stare at you as if you've got *care in the community* stamped on your forehead if you try small talk on them; and vastly superior, because they know nothing. We, out in the provinces, know all about them. We have no choice: we're force-fed their rail strikes, their arts, their personalities, their preoccupations, their scandals. But they know nothing about us. And knowledge is power.

Londoners' energies are taken up with the daily battle of living. They are insulated from the weather, the seasons, the real, natural world. They are famously inward-looking. They don't know how other people in their own city live, never mind those outside. They are disorganized, incapable of communal action. Francine says that on the one occasion she went to a Greenham Common weekend, back in the early eighties, there were as many coach loads of women from our small town and its hinterlands as from the *whole* of London. (Three, to be exact.) A lot of Londoners, I comfort myself, while I wrestle with redrawn and unfamiliar tube maps, or get lost in subways, or hear myself crying, 'Oh, look, there's Tower Bridge!' like a starry-eyed tourist, simply don't have a clue.

Now I'm in Chelsea, and here's the Embankment. The Thames and the architecture fronting it look more attractive than I remember. The stone parapets look cleaner. The river less oily. Either the environment really has improved, or I have inadvertently slipped my tourist-goggles on.

Francine told me that the block of flats couldn't be missed, because there was a ten-foot copper angel blowing a hunting-horn on a plinth in front of it. She's right, the sculpture's unmissable, though I would have called the instrument at the angel's lips a celestial trumpet, myself. Just beyond is the vehicular access to the basement car park. Half-way down this I have to stop to speak into an intercom in front of a barrier and a video camera. A disembodied voice asks for my name and car registration, tells me to wait a minute – they'll be checking against details Francine has given them – and then the barrier lifts. I enter the car park. I wonder how much service charge the tenants pay for this. You need thousands just for the simple things in life, like a guaranteed parking space, in central London.

I park, grab my small suitcase and carrier bag, and take a tiny lift to the second floor. Not a Schindler lift. This one is wood panelled and smells of furniture polish, as if it's pretending to be an antique, and makes a noise like a very quiet jet engine.

The corridor that I emerge into is also quiet. I resist the impulse to tiptoe. Flat 23 is on my right. My hand hesitates over the bellpush, decides against it, and slips the key into the lock. I step into a small squarish hallway; it is even quieter, if possible, in here. The door in front of me opens into a large dove-grey and blue sitting room. The sparse furniture is low and simple. I have no way of knowing if it is fashionable, but it looks comfortable. It looks expensive. There is a silky rectangular rug decorated with leaping dolphins in the centre of the fitted carpet. I recognize this rug – Francine brought it back from Greece a few years ago but decided, regretfully, that it didn't look right in any room in the farmhouse. Several more doors lead off this room. Two on the right, one opening into a double bedroom, the other into a bathroom, and two on the left: a galley kitchen and another bedroom. I recognize a major design fault that unaccountably pleases me: if you slept in this smaller bedroom you'd have to cross the whole of the sitting room to have a pee at night. The petition boxes that Francine has already brought up are in this smaller room, stacked behind the door. They make a brown cardboard wall eight boxes long by four high. A daunting prospect for tomorrow.

I decide to use the big front double bedroom, return to it, and put my case on the bed. This room has a view over the river. The windows must be double glazed; that's why the traffic outside sounds so distant. From my carrier bag I remove a crusty loaf of bread and a carton of eggs, wrapped in clingfilm in case of accidents, and go off to explore the kitchen.

The fittings here are stainless steel. I have never cooked in a stainless-steel kitchen before; it suggests the galley in a ship. The metal surfaces are matt and scoured-looking, like the back of a watch, and there is a workmanlike, non-domestic feel to the place. The fridge is humming and contains an opened jar of pesto sauce, a tub of Marks & Spencer sunflower margarine, and a half-full litre bottle of tonic water. In the cupboard above the silvery work surface I find tins: of ordinary foods like tomatoes and kidney beans, plus those you'd never normally buy tinned, baby potatoes, carrots, mushrooms, peas.

I can't decide whether to eat or bathe first. I seem

to be surrounded by a surfeit of potential indulgences. I decide to bathe. I go back into the bedroom to undress but get distracted, and find myself staring out of the window. The world outside does not seem to have any connection with the inner world of the flat. I can see out, but it is hard to believe that anyone out there, even if they were at my level, could see in. I wonder, very distantly, what Nick is doing at this moment. He will be already at the Foundry, I expect, preparing to play. I say this to myself, but it is just a word-thought, with no picture to go with it. Then I swing round and gaze at the interior of the room. A neat, grey and yellow underfurnished room. I imagine living here, in this pocket of limbo where nobody can touch me, for ever.

I undress and go to the bathroom. This contains a shower cubicle as well as a huge clawfoot bath; I choose the latter. I bathe quickly, dress again, and go into the kitchen to cook myself an omelette. This I stuff with tinned mushrooms and serve with tinned baby potatoes. The texture and taste of tinned potatoes is nothing like the fresh article; more like salted, unripe, waxy pears. I'm still hungry afterwards so I eat two hunks of crusty bread.

Then I return to the sitting room. There is a telephone here which Francine has said I am welcome to use – one of Lionel's companies pays the bill – but I can't think of anyone to ring. Nick isn't at home. I don't need to talk to Francine and unless she's got the cordless phone on her lap I will only be forcing her to hobble. I don't want to talk to my mother. Nor Grace; not until there are no facts to hide from her. Actually, I'm not sure I want to talk to anyone. I'm not sure I want to be forcibly located in the real world. I don't think I'd ring Nick even if he wasn't out. What would there be to say? It would just be a reminder of things unsaid.

I turn on the television – not because I genuinely want to watch anything, but because it is one of the toys of the flat and I can't resist playing with it. The news is on and I am shocked to see that world events are much the same here as they were at home. I turn the set off again. I have to admit, I'm a little restless. The flat is very warm. I feel the radiators beneath the double-glazed windows but they are cold. The windows themselves are hinged and look as if they are capable of opening, but have locks on them that I don't know how to release. I expect they require special keys. I imagine the flat hermetically sealed and wonder how long I would survive in the air it contains. I remember, for the first time in months, that I used to be asthmatic. Somewhere in my bathroom cabinet at home I still have an inhaler.

I breathe in and out several times to reassure myself that my lungs are unconstricted. I can feel my diaphragm rising and falling; the strongest muscle in the body; or is that the womb? It is possible, I daresay, for anxiety to affect your body, even when it is banished from your mind.

For something to do I go back down to the car and

carry up the two small boxes of petition forms that I brought with me. I meet no one in the corridor, the lift, or the car park. Bar the disembodied caretaker's voice, I have heard no evidence of human presence here at all – I could be the only occupant in the block, entirely alone. Time passes very slowly. There are books in the living room but I can't settle to reading. I stand at the window and watch the river darken and slowly become absorbed into the night darkness. Now only patches of surface glitter remain. By eleven I feel I have been in the flat most of my life. The sensation is familiar; this is how I used to feel in Nick's hospital: cut off, enervated, and powerless. Institutionalized. Just now, it's not an unacceptable feeling. It makes me feel less responsible. Less to blame for anything.

I get undressed and set my travel alarm for seven-thirty. I must remember to book the taxis first thing.

Chapter 10

It is 7.50 a.m. I am showering in the big bathroom, with the door closed but not locked, and I am sure someone has just entered the flat. I heard the clunk of the front door – or a noise very like it and from the right direction – and now that I am actively listening, with the water spray turned off, I can hear distant kitchen-like noises.

I remind myself that as long as I can hear these noises, and assuming that the flat has not been invaded by a gang, I can safely leave the shower cubicle and cross the floor to lock the door. This I do. I then return to the cubicle, restart the water, and rinse the shampoo from my hair.

Is this the day the maid comes? I thought Francine said that that was Monday. Perhaps, like anyone else, she occasionally alters her schedule. Who else could it be? I am more puzzled than anxious, and any anxiety I do feel is connected purely to the fact that I haven't any clothes in here. I arrived in the bathroom wrapped in a towel, and that was how I was intending to leave.

I step out of the cubicle and, while I'm drying myself, glance around the bathroom. The trouble with unlived-in apartments is that they haven't got old dressing gowns hanging behind their bathroom doors. Well. I'm dry. I can't remain hidden in here indefinitely. Whoever is in the flat must be aware of my presence. My possessions are scattered in the bedroom and sitting room, and the sound of a shower running is probably audible from both.

I listen again. My visitor is now being very quiet. I'm sure I would have heard the door if he or she had left. I wrap the bath towel around myself and tuck in the top corner firmly between my breasts. It is a good-sized towel, decently covering me from armpit to lower thigh.

I unlock the bathroom door and peer out. There are only a couple of yards to skip along the side of the sitting room to the door of my bedroom. Mid skip, a voice from the other side of the room says, 'And good morning to you.'

I know that voice. It is Lionel's. He is sitting in one of the armchairs holding a cup of coffee. His suit is grey, his shirt duck-egg blue, his tie navy; colourwise, he matches the room. He looks comfortable, perfectly centred. And satisfied. Like a man who has bankrupted several small presumptuous nations before breakfast.

'What are you doing here?' I complain, disregarding

the fact that this is his flat. 'Francine warned you we'd be here today. I remember posting the letter.' A dribble of water from my inefficiently towel-dried hair trickles down my cheek. I daren't lift my arms to wipe it away, as they are needed to keep the towel in place.

He nods, an amused but predominantly gracious gesture. 'Indeed. But she also said, when I rang her yesterday, that you'd be on your own.'

You could interpret this the wrong way. But Lionel is not, I'm sure, a dangerous man. He may be a seducer, but he is not a rapist. He has not rushed here in the hope of assaulting lone betowelled women.

'Would you care to explain?' I demand. 'Fairly quickly?' I'm actually having to force myself to sound aggressive. There is something ludicrous about the situation; it induces in me a feeling of recklessness. I imagine, just for a split second, stretching out my arms, and letting the towel fall. He has such an overconfident, arrogant face.

'I've come to help,' he says simply. 'Francine should have been here, shouldn't she? She's dropped out, so I've dropped in.'

'I see.' I stare at him. I am astonished. 'Does Francine know?'

He sips at his coffee before replying. 'I haven't told her, no.' He pauses. 'You can ring her, if you like.' He tips his head towards the telephone. 'But I used to do all this, you know. I'm sure she's told you. I'm good at interviews.'

He's offering to help deliver the petition, and deal with the media. I start to smile. This is irresistible. 'I'll get dressed,' I say, and pad on to the bedroom.

As I pull on my presentation clothes – a conventional calf-length skirt and linen jacket – I can't stop smiling. I don't care what his game is. He probably doesn't know himself yet – he is, after all, a professional risk-taker. Despite this, however, he is still a believer. And I bet he's good on television. Lionel in eco-action. I hope I'm in for a treat.

I finish dressing quickly. Emerging from the bedroom I find Lionel the far side of the sitting room, laying a small occasional table for breakfast. He sees me and pats the back of one of the chairs he has drawn up. He is inviting me to sit down, so I do. Only one place is laid. I am presented with coffee and real orange juice: Lionel must have brought it with him – and hot muffins. I don't stand on ceremony, or on dignity. I recognize a male in pampering mood, and this is my kind of breakfast. Lionel pours himself another cup of coffee and sits down beside me.

When I've finished the first muffin and am buttering the second, he says, 'I admire a woman who eats. There's something very . . . atavistic about it.'

Good heavens, he does start early in the morning. 'Be something very dead about one who didn't,' I say cheerfully.

Lionel sips his coffee.

After a minute I say, 'Got to ring for taxis. To leave

here at ten, or thereabouts.' I lick a sticky finger. These muffins are glorious. Crisp on the outside with a soft, doughy heart. The strawberry jam isn't bad, either.

'I've done it,' says Lionel. 'Main foyer, ten o'clock. We'll have to take the boxes down in the lift.'

Thank goodness there is a lift, I think. I haven't yet, this morning, given thought to moving the boxes from bedroom to taxis. The weak link. What Nick was meant to be here for. Lionel's help will be useful, there's no denying it. He has beautiful cufflinks, I notice. You don't see many men wearing cufflinks these days. Dark-blue stones set in gold. The stones have a swirling appearance, like tiny universes. Nick hasn't got any cufflinks at all, as far as I'm aware.

After we've cleared away the breakfast plates Lionel asks to be briefed. I find him a copy of the press release. 'Three million signatures,' I say. 'From forty countries. Primary forest hosts were co-sponsors.'

'Why are we presenting this now?' His eyes skim the press release.

'Because of the UN conference in August. We want resolutions tabled. We can't lobby anyone except our own PM.'

'Right.' After a minute Lionel folds the sheet and tucks it into his jacket pocket. 'I've got all I need.'

I go off to pack my suitcase, so it's ready when I come back for the car, and soon it's time to move the boxes. Lionel turns out to be worth the help of two men over this, not a mere one, because he knows how to press buttons on the telephone to summon the caretaker. The caretaker has keys to a service lift, much larger and more hold-like than the passenger lift. I don't have to do anything; they carry the boxes down between them.

The air outside the flats is warmer and more humid than it was inside and the sun is a pale yellow orb in a misty grey sky. The gods are smiling on us; it's going to be a hot, fine day. Our two taxis arrive within five minutes and we divide the boxes between the vehicles. Or rather, Lionel and the drivers do. I feel as if I have a team of men working expressly for me, a conceit Lionel encourages with his announcement to the drivers that, 'My lady colleague has a petition to deliver to the Prime Minister.'

In the back of the leading taxi, walled in with boxes and alone – Lionel is following in the second cab – my knees begin to ache. Nick will be at the shop by now. He won't have to leave for the hospital till around 2.30. Though he may go earlier, since he's on his own, and won't want to feel any time pressure. I hope he has queues of customers this morning. I hope Jason is in good form. I'm glad I'm not there. What cancer puts you through is unacceptable. This is why I'm not accepting it.

In no time at all we are in Westminster. The Houses of Parliament appear on my right, looking astonishingly scrubbed and clean. The pavements are full of ambling or queuing multi-hued tourists, men in purposeful dark suits, and watchful police officers. We continue past Westminster Bridge and into the wide expanse of Parliament Street, and pull up just inside Richmond Terrace, directly opposite the entrance to Downing Street. I climb out and start unloading my boxes on to the pavement, until Lionel's taxi draws up behind and he stops me. He and the drivers do the rest. Uniformed police officers at the barrier across the road are watching us and speaking into their radios. I stare down the carriageway. You can see a long way down – or is it up? – Parliament Street. The sun has burnt the morning mist away and the first sharp shadows have appeared. I can see our volunteer helpers. A tree is approaching on the pavement. That is, a man dressed as a tree. He is fruiting heavily and the trunk is tight around his knees so his progress is slow. Behind him, dressed more conventionally, though still in greens and browns, are two young men pushing a large foliage-bedecked trolley.

'Hi,' the tree says, as he approaches. 'You must be Demeter.'

'Yes,' I agree. 'Jess.' His fruits are a variety of sustainable forest products, from nuts and replicas of genuine fruits to rubber erasers and medicine bottles that say things like *curare*.

The tree stares at Lionel. Lionel does not look like an average environmental protester. He looks more like a prime minister.

'Lionel Brackenbury?' the tree asks. There's a child-like gape on his face/trunk.

Lionel nods and says, 'Pleased to meet you.' He includes the two trolley-pushers in his welcome. Everyone is too polite and democratic to cry, 'Hey, we got Lionel Brackenbury to present the petition!' but the enthusiasm in their expressions says it for them. Lionel is one of the environmental movement's recognizable faces – within the movement, that is. He is renowned as a dynamic initiator. Most people still see him as that, not as a power-hungry opportunist who's since moved on, or, indeed, as an absent, impossible husband. I fantasize pleasantly about the effect I could have if I piped up with, 'Yes, he's divorcing Francine and for some reason thinks this'll really get up her nose.' Of course I wouldn't dream of saying it.

The two young men load the trolley and tug a leaf-decorated net over the bare cardboard of the boxes. By now a gaggle of men with cameras and trailing wires who can only be the press have collected the other side of the road. At least one television company is here – I spot the shoulder-borne camera and furry broom-head microphone. A small crowd of supporters is drifting up too. A woman with long fair hair and a clipboard – one of the Day of Action marshals, I assume – gives us a cheerful wave.

After a few minutes Lionel looks at his watch and says, 'Now, I think.' Some silent pantomime between him and the police opposite results in two officers stepping obediently into the road to stop the traffic. We could probably have managed the crossing on our own, but police assistance is always welcome. It has a legitimizing effect. I am beginning to grasp a truth about Lionel: he has such absolute belief in his own power, and his right to exert it, that others – caretakers, taxi drivers, policemen, accept it too. His aura says *I am a leader of men (and women), obey me.* And we do.

The police have a list of persons who will be allowed through the barrier into Downing Street to present the petition, and this list does not include individuals dressed as trees. Any of those hanging fruits could be a bomb, I suppose. So the tree will remain outside and entertain the press. We don't argue because this arrangement is probably what we would have chosen anyway. The actual moment of petition presentation is always a let down: everyone knows that the PM himself will not be opening the door of No. 10 and receiving it. He is, indeed, today, not even in residence.

The trolley is cleared by the police and we proceed into Downing Street. The buildings either side are tall with continuous façades and the whole street is in deep, cool shadow. Before presenting the petition we stop and have our photos taken. Lionel poses for the camera as if he does so daily. I expect, like Nick, he is very photogenic.

Then a policeman arranges for the door of No. 10

to open and we hand over the boxes and petition letter to an aide. The transfer takes five minutes, and that's it; the door closes. As we walk back to the barrier one of our helpers whispers to me, 'They'll be stored in the cellar. The last anyone will see of them.' He sounds amused by this, however, not depressed.

In our absence the tree has been posing for the cameras, and now it is our turn. The blonde woman with the clipboard bustles up. 'Just down there, they've suggested,' she says, pointing to where a cameraman and sound engineer are aiming their instruments at a colleague. 'We could make a lunchtime slot,' she says. 'Possibly again early evening, if they do a round-up.'

Lionel nods. She is, of course, addressing him. She hasn't asked who is speaking for us; why else would he be here?

He strides over to the television group. He has, he says in a strong, authoritative voice, a statement to make. Immediately a bright light comes on, and the furry broom-head is pushed forward.

Lionel addresses his speech to the Prime Minister, calling him the 'the most powerful man in Britain'. He doesn't, of course, believe this. That politicians hold ultimate power, that is. Like Francine, he believes it resides in big business, which is why he is a business man. But never mind.

After a brief background to the petition, and a list of our rights and demands – my, he does make us environmentalists sound important – he proceeds to explain the ecological importance of forests, with great clarity. Their effect on climate, on the physical stability of the earth beneath their roots. That they are the last scientifically unexplored region above the oceans, and the richest in life forms. That we are destroying – irrevocably – the gene pool, and the lungs, of the world. That forests are not uninhabited, though it may suit governments, as they turn blind eyes to the genocidal effects of exploitation, to pretend they are. All the usual stuff, but articulated with great force and freshness. He says that at the current rate of destruction all primary rainforest will be gone in three decades. Thirty years. An entirely unnecessary, man-made, ecological and human catastrophe.

'We will be alive for this,' he warns. 'You,' – he indicates the television journalist – 'will be, what, sixty? I will be over seventy. This is more than a terrible vandalistic legacy for our children . . .'

He will be nearer eighty, surely? Amazing man. Even in the passion of the moment he doesn't forget to improve on his own image. I step back, look at my watch, and feel my knees ache again. For nearly an hour I have forgotten Nick. If I wanted to, I could rush off now. The presentation has taken less time than I imagined. I could flag down a taxi, pick up the car within fifteen minutes, and be out of London by noon. I could; but I'm not going to.

A woman beside me murmurs, 'He's good, isn't

he?' staring at Lionel. She's looking at him the way nice women stare at male strippers. Half appalled, half mesmerized.

Then Lionel's speech is over, and our part in the day's activity has ended. A sense of achievement lightens the air. Lionel smiles at everyone in an indulgent, headmasterly way. The press pack up and we start to move down the road. Going somewhere, in the direction of Parliament Square. I've forgotten exactly where.

'The Grand Committee Room,' someone tells me. 'The speeches. And you should try to lobby your MP, too.'

I remember: there is to be a mass lobby in the afternoon. The main event of the Day. I definitely can't stay for that.

Lionel comes alongside. I'm sure he has no intention of going to the speeches. You have to queue outside the Palace to get into the Grand Committee Room and submit to metal detection sweeps and personal searches. No press will be there. Not a place for Lionel.

He takes my elbow. 'Lunch, I think,' he says.

I let myself be steered aside. Well, I wasn't really intending to go to the Palace, was I? And, whatever my plans, I will need lunch some time.

Lionel has already said his adieus. A few hands are raised as we detach ourselves from the group. A busy man, Lionel. Everyone understands. I won't be missed at all.

A taxi materializes under Lionel's flicked fingers and we climb in. We sit back and chug away from the action.

'Well,' I say, after a moment, 'you enjoyed that, didn't you?'

Lionel smiles, as if he is proud of me. A patronizing smile, to top my patronizing remark.

'I did, as it happens. And why not?'

'I wasn't complaining.'

'No,' says Lionel. 'You were provoking.'

He might as well have said *You were flirting*. Was I? Am I? Am I not enjoying the attentions of this preposterous man? Am I not feeling that I could bury myself in them?

I push answers, decisions, away from me. I am just going to have lunch with him.

After ten minutes or so the taxi stops somewhere I can't immediately identify. But we must be near Piccadilly Circus because a moment ago we were in the Haymarket; I recognized the leaping horses statue on the corner. We have parked in a narrow backstreet. The slender mews-type houses look like private residences, though I'm sure they aren't.

'Up here,' says Lionel, guiding me through a doorway. We ascend uncarpeted wooden stairs to a plain mirrored lobby, and then we're in a restaurant. There is a small bar lit with green-shaded lamps and, beyond, half a dozen white-clothed tables. At the far end of the room are two lumpy sofas either side of a deep, tapestry-screened fireplace. A delicate gold-faced clock inside a gold-and-glass belljar sits on the mantelpiece above. That end of the room could be someone's private house. If that someone was very well off.

The place is quiet. We are early – it is only just twelve. A middle-aged couple are sipping aperitifs at the bar and two men are talking quietly at a table, with no food as yet in front of them.

A woman with shoulder-length black hair in a navy suit asks if she can take my jacket. Her smile suggests we are very welcome friends. Lionel calls her Hetty. The atmosphere feels quietly relaxed.

Lionel asks what I would like to drink and I say, 'I don't know, surprise me.' I have a sudden intuition that the way to treat this man is to use his strengths. He is a decisionmaker – let him decide everything.

We are taken to a table in one of the window alcoves and two tall straight clinking glasses are brought over. I think mine is gin and vermouth. I admire the damask napkins and tablecloth.

'Is this place a club?' I ask.

'No.' Lionel rotates his glass in his large fingers.

'What, you mean anyone could eat here?'

He shrugs. 'If they knew about it. If there was a table.'

'Ah.' I sit back to let Hetty deliver menus. Lionel doesn't pick his up. I do.

This is a man's restaurant. I can tell from the puddings. They've even got spotted dick. They call it 'currant pudding'. And bread and butter pudding. Also I can understand all the earlier sections of the menu. Plain meat and fish, British vegetables. Boiled silverside of beef, with carrots and onions. Poached salmon and lemon sauce. Buttered parsnips. The vegetarian dishes are Stilton cheese flan and poached eggs on spinach. I close the menu folder; I only looked at it for fun. Lionel the Decision-Maker can choose.

He seems delighted to do this. Temporarily, I realize, we are perfectly compatible. The young waitress who comes to take our order wears an Alice band and looks like an escapee from a girls' public school. She will be called Arabella, or Henrietta, or Fenella.

'I like plain food,' Lionel says. 'I assume you're happy with that?'

'I eat anything,' I say. 'Except licorice, because I once made myself ill on it. Oh, and I hate the taste of cola.'

Lionel murmurs, 'How refreshing,' and without any reference to the menu orders mutton – which I don't think I've ever before eaten in this country – with mint sauce, broccoli and braised onions, and new potatoes. He also orders a bottle of red wine.

I don't stop him doing this. He is taking the decisions. I don't say, *Not for me, Lionel, I'm driving.* I let him fill my glass. The mutton, when it arrives, is delicious. The texture is tenderly fibrous and it tastes . . . well, it tastes, sweetly and authentically, of mature sheep. I drink my wine and let Lionel refill the glass.

And again. There is a point after which things slip away from you. For pudding we have ginger sponge with dollops of real custard. We hardly talk. The alcohol has dulled the ache in my knees. I have a small sensation of pressure in my chest, but I am successfully ignoring it.

We have finished our meal by one-thirty. I do not see Lionel pay the bill but perhaps he has an account. My jacket is returned to me and at the bottom of the wooden stairway we find yet another taxi waiting for us. Lionel gives the driver the Embankment flat address, and we both get in. I do not query the fact that he appears to be coming back with me. I want him to. I want him to continue to be in charge. I can hide very successfully in him.

We sit beside each other in the taxi and I wait, patiently, for him to make some sort of advance. What else is all this about?

Eventually it comes. He leans slightly in my direction and says in a steady, bedroom voice, 'Your boyfriend. He's a lucky man.'

This is so untrue, so perfectly, absolutely wrong, this particular day, that I give a whoop of laughter.

Lionel tucks his chin into his neck. 'Should I understand the joke?'

'No.' I stop laughing and shake my head. 'You shouldn't. I'm sorry.' I speak sincerely. I don't want to annoy Lionel. He is being very useful. 'Thank you for lunch,' I say. And I turn to him, deliberately, and smile.

He is encouraged. 'I bet,' he says in a low voice, 'that you are very interesting in bed.'

I continue to smile at him. I wonder if he is? You hear tales about public-school business men. Perhaps he likes being tied up and spanked? Lectured by females in gym slips? Or, like so many womanizers, does he in fact despise women, and want to hurt them? I immediately dismiss this last idea. If Lionel had been a sexual sadist Francine – who can be surprisingly indiscreet about intimate matters – would have told me. It would have figured in the catalogue of his crimes.

Lionel takes my hand and strokes it. He pinches the flesh at the base of my thumb. The action is deeply sensual. Lionel would not touch a woman's breasts or slip a hand up her skirt in the back of a taxi, but both are suggested in the caress. I let him arouse me. Skin is an erogenous zone – it hardly matters, when the imagination is switched on and unconstrained, where it is stimulated. For a short while there is still a window out: a time when I can contemplate the question *who is using whom?* and could conceivably, depending on the answer, back out. But then it passes.

Chapter 11

We make love in the sitting room of the flat. Lionel does not ask to be tied up or spanked, nor require me to wear a gym slip. He is gently assertive but not pushy. He sits on one of the chairs with me astride him, and he asks what makes me come before we get going; and manages to do it right and delay his own climax till after mine. At nearly fifty, with as much practice as, reputedly, he has had, the least you would expect is competence. His naked body is not as firm as Nick's but there is more bulk to it. His flesh is whiter. He has a solid barrel chest you could beat your fists against and he'd scarcely feel it.

He is probably disappointed in me. From his earlier remarks I suspect he had hoped for a gymnastic, or at least spirited, performance. I am capable of both but am not inclined on this occasion. I have my own agenda. I am responsive, and prepared to show pleasure, but take no initiatives.

However, if he is disappointed, he doesn't show it. He is affectionate and complimentary afterwards. Solicitous and gentlemanly. The fact of my seduction is probably more important to him than the mechanics of it, or the transitory pleasure it provides. The fact of it will be a lasting satisfaction.

I am slightly disappointed in him. Or in the event, rather. He is a little too practised, too organized, too gentlemanly for my purposes. I would have preferred evidence that the outside world is more random, more impulsively hit-or-miss. More heartless and relentless. Even callous. In my mind Lionel can be the personification of forces beyond my control, to which I can give myself up; in real life he is a middle-aged, occasionally decent, occasionally principled man and cannot know the peculiarity of my desires.

We take a shower afterwards and it must be the white bathroom tiles around us that remind me of hospitals. It's probably about 3.30. Nick may be with the consultant right now.

I step out of the shower, start to say something to Lionel, and realize that I am wheezing. I haven't wheezed for five years. I no longer carry my inhaler with me.

Lionel is still soaping himself and singing in a melodic baritone voice. He's only dum-de-dumming but I recognize the tune: it's Queen's '*We are the Champions*'. He's the right age to be a fan; or maybe it's taught to business men on positive-thinking courses.

'Lionel,' I say, and get his attention immediately, 'I think I'm going to have an asthma attack.'

His small whale-eyes boggle at me. He has foam on his head and shoulders and streaked down his broad chest. Some men would look ludicrous like this, as if they'd just had the washing-up poured over their heads. Lionel looks in his element.

He steps out of the shower, wraps a towel around his middle, and says, 'I'll get you a dressing gown.' He leaves the room and returns very quickly with a white fleecy wrap. Like the one Francine was wearing in hospital. She must have clothes stored here somewhere. He helps me put it on and guides me into the sitting room.

'Now,' he says, sounding not at all panicky, 'what do you need?'

I'm not panicking either, yet. 'My inhaler. Something like Ventolin.' I don't know if it's still used, these days. Drugs move on, change names.

'Is Ventolin a prescription drug?'

'It used to be. Yes, I'm sure it is.'

'Right.' Lionel has dropped his towel and is pulling on clothes. 'There are doctors in the block. Several two doors away. I'll see who's around.'

He finishes dressing and leaves. I go to stand at the window and rest my hands on the sill, concentrating on holding my shoulders apart. I can exhale more easily standing than sitting. With asthma, breathing out is the problem, not breathing in. You wheeze on exhalation, not inhalation.

Lionel is gone barely two minutes. He returns accompanied by a tall youngish man with floppy hair and a goofy smile, wearing a dark green collar-less shirt and baggy cream trousers. I turn from the window.

'Jessica,' Lionel says, introducing us. 'This is James. James, Jessica feels she is about to have an asthma attack.'

James takes my hand and shakes it. I say, 'Hello. Are you really a doctor?' And what kind of doctor, I wonder, and why isn't he at work?

James smiles. He is a doctor. He's listening to my breathing.

Lionel says, 'James is a registrar from Leicester. He shares the flat down the corridor with three colleagues. It's . . .' his lips curve, 'their London pad.'

James's smile becomes a loose grin. It occurs to me that he's been drinking. Possibly more than Lionel and I have. Doctors work hard, and play hard. But he doesn't look incapable.

'Are you well otherwise?' he asks. I nod.

'Not on any other medication?'

'Only the Pill.'

'And you've had asthma before, have you?'

'A while ago.' Talking isn't too difficult. Having a doctor standing in front of me does open my chest a little. But only a little.

'And you used to take, what? Bricanol? Ventolin?'

'Ventolin.'

He seems satisfied. 'Have you got a pad?' he asks Lionel. 'And a pen? I'll write a prescription.'

Lionel gives him a gold pen from his inside pocket and searches furniture drawers until he finds some plain writing paper. He slaps it on top of one of the small tables.

'It'll be a sealed unit,' says James, glancing at me while leaning over the table to write. 'There won't be separate capsules. OK?'

'OK,' I say.

We wait while he finishes writing. He gives the prescription to Lionel and then taps his lower lip with the gold pen.

'The nearest chemist . . .' he says, 'is, I think . . .'

'I know where it is,' says Lionel. 'Give me ten minutes. Can you stay with her?'

'I can indeed.' James gives me a charming smile.

Lionel says, 'Ten, at the outside,' to me, and leaves. James and I continue to smile at each other. I still don't want to sit down, but I don't think James will unless I do. We can't stand smiling at each other for ten minutes. Unfortunately there is no chair here that will give me the right easy breathing position. I move back and perch on a sofa arm. That's better. From here I can brace myself on the adjacent table. James sits down in one of the armchairs. When I catch his eye he grins boyishly at me. His face is flushed. He must be about my age. My and Nick's age. Maybe a little older.

I get the feeling that the constriction in my chest will ease if I squeeze something out. I have a doctor here to listen to me, totally concentrating on me.

I say, 'I think it's partly worry. My boyfriend has cancer.'

James looks alarmed. His eyes flick at the door.

'No, no,' I say. 'Lionel's not my boyfriend.'

'Ah.' James doesn't know what to say. He's staring at my dressing gown. He starts to smile but then decides against it.

'At home,' I say. 'My boyfriend. He has malignant melanoma.'

James frowns. 'Poor man.'

Of course I didn't expect him to toss the news over his shoulder, as if it were salt. He may be half-cut, but he's still a doctor.

'A year ago,' I say. I can hear the wheeze in my voice now. 'He had an operation. We've been anxious, you know, ever since.'

'A year ago?' James's face relaxes. 'And you're still worried?'

I stare at him.

'Malignant melanoma is a very aggressive cancer,' James says. 'It spreads jolly quickly. Straight to lymph and liver, usually. Really bad news. But if it was a year ago . . . I'd relax. Honestly. They must have removed it all. If he wasn't cured by now, he'd be dead.'

I find it hard to move. James steeples his fingers.

He's into his stride, starting to sound like a textbook. 'The prognosis depends on how young the tumour is when it is removed. How deep it has got. If you catch it before cells break off from underneath and travel, well, you know, you're OK. If you don't . . well . . . obviously that's a different matter. But it's a notoriously fastmoving cancer. You should know either way by now.'

I have learnt more about the progression of malignant melanoma in the last half minute than in the whole of last year. None of Nick's doctors told us this. Well, none of his doctors told *me* anything; I never saw them. If they told Nick he was either too shocked, or too ill, to grasp what they were saying. I have learnt the facts quite fortuitously, from an inebriated stranger.

I'd like to leave the conversation there, but I can't.

'He's gone to the hospital today,' I say. 'He had a lump. They took a biopsy. Today he gets the result.'

James's expression has frozen. He may have shot his mouth off too soon.

'Where is this lump?' he asks.

I indicate my forearm. James pulls a face and murmurs, 'Unlikely.' But he doesn't say 'impossible'. I hate seeing him retreat like this, but I am impelled to continue.

'One of the lymph glands under his arm was swollen, too.'

James is not looking at me now. Something below

the window has caught his attention. 'There are dozens of reasons why lymph glands swell. Some people are very sensitive. Any minor infection does it.'

There is a short silence. I would have difficulty saying anything now even if I wanted to. My breath is whistling. James can hear it too.

'I'll make you some strong coffee,' he says, jumping up. 'That helps a bit.'

He sounds efficient in the kitchen. He returns carrying a jug and pours me a cupful. The coffee is black. He tells me to hold the cup close to my mouth between sips, so I'll get the benefit of the steam as well as the caffeine. He's right, I remember my own doctor telling me that coffee is a broncho-dilator.

After a few sips I can speak again. I say, 'What I just told you. About my boyfriend. Please don't tell Lionel.'

James inclines his head. 'Of course not.' He is a doctor, the nod says; naturally our conversation was private.

Before I finish the coffee Lionel is back. I put down the mug and snatch the paper bag he holds out to me. Inside is the inhaler. I remove the safety plastic, hold the device to my mouth, puff, and inhale. The effect is magical. I exhale. I can, suddenly, exhale. James and Lionel smile, first at me, then at each other. They look delighted. I'm something they've solved, that's gone right for them. Oh, I'm lucky. A doctor one side, Lionel the other. I might never worry my head about anything, ever again.

I leave the men congratulating each other and pouring out the rest of the coffee for themselves, and retire to the bedroom. My intention is to dress, but once I've closed the door the impulse leaves me. I get as far as taking off the fleecy dressing gown and then stop. I stare out of the window. I am in here, naked, in this dead-aired limbo-flat, while outside is bright and alive with afternoon sunlight, and I am suddenly, crushingly, exhausted.

I lie down on top of the bed quilt. It is too hot in this flat. I close my eyes. I experience a falling sensation, which is not unpleasant. With my eyes still closed I fantasize a future where I lie here forever, deep in this bed – in this bed that suddenly feels more like a cot – in this insulating womb of a flat. Where Lionel, or some other strong, organizing, horizon-filling being visits at intervals to feed and water and wash and look after me. I have nothing to do. No duties or responsibilities. I have totally, willingly withdrawn.

The last thing I remember is my own fingertips brushing my opposite upper arm, and imagining that Nick's cat has come back to see me. I can even hear his distant purr.

Chapter 12

It is light. Something is trilling. I am in an unfamiliar, warm room.

A soft satin-edged blanket slides from my body as I push myself up. It wasn't here when I lay down; someone has come in to the bedroom and covered me.

I identify the trilling as the phone at the moment the noise stops. I reach for my watch: just after seven. Lionel is talking next door, but I can't hear what he is saying.

I swing my legs off the bed and start to pull on clothes. Travelling clothes this time: trousers and a T-shirt. I never normally sleep during the day and my body hates it – my muscles feel flaccid and incompetent. My brain is sluggish. I keep thinking that I am about to wake up. I open my eyes very wide and remind myself that I am already awake. I can't hear Lionel's voice any longer. The taste in my mouth is disgusting, as if I have been chewing fur. I need to wash my teeth, or drink something. I open the bedroom door.

Lionel is on his own. He is sitting reading a broadsheet newspaper with his feet up on the coffee table, wearing a pair of wire-framed reading glasses. He looks domestic; almost fatherly.

'Ah,' he says, turning to me and removing the glasses. 'That was for you. Sorry. I told them you were asleep.'

'Who was it?'

'A man. Says he'll ring back later.'

I walk through to the kitchen, pour myself the last of the fridge milk, and return to the sitting room drinking it.

'You sleep like a boy,' Lionel says.

'Seen many boys asleep, have you?'

Lionel is amused. 'Yes, actually. You forget I went to boarding school. And I have a son. Girls' – he corrects himself – '. . . women, curl up into themselves. Boys spread their limbs out.'

The nature of the sexes, he might have said. What tosh. I sip the milk. Just because he wants me to know that he covered me up without disturbing me. Or touching me. I don't care. He should have invited the street in. Why should I mind? I was asleep.

The phone call must have been from Nick. I am paralysed, muzzily, between the desire to be here when he rings again, and the desire not to be. Seeing things from his point of view is difficult. I'm trying to imagine what would be going through my mind if I had just been told the result of a crucial biopsy, and my girlfriend, my partner, who had promised to share the experience with me as soon as she could get away from a prior commitment, mysteriously didn't turn up. And what would I feel when I got so anxious that, as a long shot, I rang the number of the last place she'd been, and was told by an unfamiliar male voice that she was indeed there, but was asleep? At seven in the evening?

I would start, I think, now I was reassured that she had not had to be cut out of her car on the motorway by the emergency services, to feel rather upset. And confused. Somewhere on the scale from simply confused, to very upset.

My reaction might, of course, depend on what the result of the biopsy had been.

No, perhaps not. Or only in degree. If I had just learnt that I was likely to die (which is what I would assume if told the lump was malignant, whatever the doctor's protestations) I might be in a state of shock. I might be more frightened than upset. I might feel more needy. More deserted.

I put the empty glass down with a bang on the coffee table and pace to the window.

'Problems?' Lionel asks.

'No.' I'm not sure how much he knows about Nick. They've never met, but each knows of the other's existence. Lionel mentioned Nick, if not by name, in the taxi coming here. He has guessed that the phone call was from him. I doubt he knows about Nick's cancer. James, I'm sure, won't have broken confidence and even if Celia, say, had mentioned it in the past, the knowledge would be stored away – if it was retained at all – as yesterday's news. That's what everyone else has done with it.

If Lionel wasn't here I might consider ringing Nick myself. But Lionel mustn't know about the cancer, or the biopsy, or that today was – is – a terror day. I don't want to give him the satisfaction of feeling that he is part of our crisis. I want to know that I have used him, without him knowing it. He doesn't deserve higher billing.

I have managed to avoid taking decisions for most of the day but I am reaching a point where one is being forced on me. A partial decision, anyway.

'I have to go soon,' I say. I don't say *go home* or *go* anywhere. But I can't stay here indefinitely.

'Shall we eat first?' Lionel doesn't query my decision. No doubt it suits him that I am not planning to alter my life for him. I am the perfect seducee. A minor challenge transformed to willing participant, and no price to be paid.

I am going to have to tell Francine about having sex with him. Preferably before he tells her; which he certainly will. I watch Lionel as he gets up and strolls to the kitchen – yes, he's assumed we will eat first – and feel momentarily shaken by what we have done. What I have done. Letting this man, my employer's husband, a man I scarcely know, remove my clothes, handle my body, and enter me. That I agreed to this – no, more, connived at it. I must leave this place. This careless, complicated, dissociated, amoral place.

But I do stay long enough to eat. Tinned prawns and artichoke hearts on toast. With iced tap water. And afterwards, as I'm helping Lionel clear dishes, the phone rings again. This is Lionel's flat and he's nearest, so I can't stop him answering. He says, 'Yes?' then listens, and holds the receiver out to me.

I take it and say, 'Hello?'

'Who is that man?' It is Nick, though he sounds unfamiliar.

'Lionel.' I glance over my shoulder. Lionel is tactfully withdrawing into the kitchen.

I wait until he has gone. 'Francine's Lionel. He owns the flat.'

'What's happening?' Nick asks. As baldly as that. I am flummoxed. What is happening? How do I answer this? *I am running away from you?* Or perhaps *I'm trying to hurt you?* Or *I'm in denial?* Or, *I'm refusing to play along with the cancer.* Or no, I've got it, *I'm showing the cancer I don't care.*

In the end none of these seem possible and I simply say, 'I don't know. I'm sorry.'

There is a short perplexed silence. Then Nick says, 'Are you coming home?'

I start to feel faint. Nick is pushing me further than

I have thought myself. The words: *it depends* form in my mind, but I don't get a chance to say them.

'I was told you were in bed when I rang.'

No, I think to myself, you were told I was asleep. But if I correct him, it will suggest a lie. It will be a truth that lies. He deserves to know everything.

'Yes,' I say.

There is another silence.

'This is what you want, is it?' Nick sounds bitter. 'Why didn't you warn me?'

'I didn't know,' I whisper. 'I swear, I didn't know.'

'I thought you'd had an accident,' he says in a very low voice.

'I'm sorry.' What else can I say?

There is an even longer silence. I am waiting for him to tell me what happened at the hospital, and the result of the biopsy, but I can't ask. He knows this, I can tell from the silence. It seems to be ticking. Then a roaring sound rises behind it, as I realize what I have set myself up for.

'Nick?' I say. I implore. It's as far as I can go.

He says, 'I can't take this,' and puts the phone down.

I listen to the dialling tone, and then put my own receiver down. He knows he hasn't told me. By not telling me he is saying, what? That I have forfeited the right to know? That not knowing will be my punishment?

Lionel returns. I look at my watch: getting on for eight.

'I must go now.'

'Right you are.'

He smiles, and I find I can smile back. Since we sat down to eat a settled, platonic feeling has crept into the space between us. I can't imagine now making love with this man. It is as if, having done it once, we have exorcised our respective demons. We both got what we wanted, and neither of us needs more. I feel no disapproval of his motives. Mine take more explaining.

I collect my things and say goodbye. Lionel sees me to the lift; he offers to come down to the car park with me but I tell him not to. In the basement the Golf is parked where I left it and when I start it up the controls feel strange and spindly and as if I haven't driven the car for weeks.

It is still light out on the streets, and it will be for a while. Although I have made no decision about my destination, I find myself following signs to the M4. That's where my automatic pilot takes me.

I am on the motorway in less than fifteen minutes. I look inside myself, pin myself down, and realize that I have made a decision. At least for tonight. Another partial, procrastinating decision. I will visit my mother.

My mother lives in a brick and stucco Spanish-style bungalow on a small tidy estate on the outskirts of

Reading. The bungalow has never been my home – my mother bought it less than five years ago – and it is not a property I would wish to live in, as it was suburban and unattractive to begin with, and my mother has made it more so. As with her clothes, my mother goes for the twee, fussy look. On the brick gate posts either side of her driveway sit concrete pigs. I know these pigs are popular garden ornaments, but other people place them on terraces, or by ponds or swimming pools. No one else mounts them on gate pedestals, as if they were lions. She didn't do it as a joke; she simply thinks pigs – or piglets rather, since they sit less than eighteen inches high – are cute. The glass panes of the bungalow's double-glazed, plastic-framed windows are criss-crossed with fake leading. She is fanatical about security and so has proximity lights, masquerading as brass coaching lamps, attached at intervals to all the outside whipped-cream walls of the building. They certainly deter; on occasions when I've arrived at night the sudden view of the place in the flood-lit glare has made me feel like turning straight around and leaving again.

Tonight I arrive still in daylight. I turn into the drive, sweep past the two white non-functional wooden wheelbarrows from which tumble puce-bloomed Busy Lizzies and fuschias, and park the car. The time is just past nine; the sun is setting and the last rays have painted everything peach. Peach is one of my mother's favourite colours.

I ring the bungalow doorbell. The chime is two-tone,

but mercifully plays no recognizable tune. From inside I hear a click – a door being opened or closed – and then my mother's footsteps.

I experience the most curious physical sensation. As if my internal structure, the rigid, bracing parts of my body, my very scaffolding, is breaking up. I am being unboned.

The door opens and I say a word I haven't uttered for decades. Since I was at primary school. I say, 'Mummy.' And begin to weep.

Chapter 13

I now have evidence – as if I needed it – that my mother's helplessness is a life-style decision, not an inescapable character trait.

To restore strength to weakened others, so that those others can return to a competent state fit to be leant on, producing decisions she can then defer to, my mother needs, paradoxically, to be capable of taking charge and acting with great competence herself.

The competent, capable thing to do when your grown-up daughter arrives unexpectedly weeping on your doorstep, is to cry, 'Jessica, my dear! Why didn't you ring? Don't cry dear, you're here now,' and draw her inside. Which my mother does. She then clucks around trying to sound ineffectual but in fact checking that my car is locked, and pouring me a stiff sweet Cinzano Bianco, which is the only alcohol she keeps in the house. And she doesn't ask me anything at all until I've blown my nose several times and sipped the drink and she's found me a box of tissues and carried my overnight bag down the corridor to her spare bedroom.

Then she sits down beside me on the gold velour sofa, clasps her hands together in her lap, tilts her head towards me, and broaches the matter. As mothers do. Like a real mother. She says, 'Now, tell me what the matter is, dear.'

And I do. I tell her everything. Almost everything. I tell her that I have run away from Nick. That I have deserted him. That, actually, I was running from his cancer, but the effect is that I deserted him. That I have been afraid he might be trying to run away from me. Or not trying, but by leaving me behind, growing away from me, achieve it anyway. That today was a terror day, the third we've had since he was out of hospital – without counting the fear-tainted run-up days – and I funked it. And it's still a terror day, because Nick rang me in London and wouldn't tell me the result of the biopsy he's just had. And there's more, there's more. That all along, all this last year, I've felt alone. That I've had no one to talk to, no one to turn to. People either don't want to know, or they do – like Nick's Dad – but I've felt I should protect them, and so haven't been open about my feelings and have blocked off what might have been an outlet. When it's your best friend who's ill, and he's the person you're terrified for, who do you lean on? Who do you confide in? I used to confide in Toby, but then he died on us. Everyone else's lives seem to be progressing, going somewhere, except ours. Except mine.

My mother has no answers, except to be motherly. She says, 'There, there, poor Jessica. Poor Jessica,' taking my hands in hers and squeezing them.

Her motherliness breaks more scaffolding inside me. I can think of other grievances, other miseries. I must tell her about them, this might never happen again.

'And Celia,' I sob. 'Francine's daughter. She's round at the shop pestering Nick all the time. She makes me feel so . . . ugly.'

'Oh dear,' murmurs my mother. She takes this seriously; feeling ugly, everyone knows, is dreadful.

'I had to buy a new coat because of her.' My eyes refill with tears.

'I think you're tired,' says my mother. 'Very, very tired.'

'No one came to see him,' I say. 'When he came out of hospital. No one, except Jason.'

'It was the summer,' my mother says. 'It's a terrible time for crises. Holidays, visitors. Everyone's coming and going. And people are frightened of serious illness. Especially cancer. None of us are very brave. When your Grandad died Mummy saw two friends run away from her in Marks and Spencers. I remember her coming home in tears. The most unlikely people turn out to be the most help. That funny woman across the road, d'you remember? Asked her lots of questions about Daddy. Let her talk. You can't tell with people. Some can cope, some can't. The trouble with you' – she pats my hand with a smile – 'is that you look as if you don't want help.'

'That's not true.' I'm indignant. How can she say that?

'You always have, darling. Even when you were little. I can manage. I'm not upset. I can cope. I'm strong enough. Everything's fine.'

I am forced to swallow this because, although I want to deny it, I know I can't. It's perfectly true. I hate feeling vulnerable. I won't show it. And why should I? I feel mulish, pushed into another tack. 'What help could anyone give, anyway?'

My mother pats my hand again. 'This sort of help. Letting you unburden yourself.'

'But you thought he was going to die. Everyone did. No one had faith. I didn't want to talk to people who thought he was going to die.'

'They didn't, darling. Well,' my mother corrects herself, 'some may, I suppose. But I didn't. It's just the way you interpret things. I wanted to help. I offered you rests. Time away, if you needed it. That's not the same as thinking Nick was going to die. I was worried about you. But you didn't want to know. You pushed everything away. You assumed the worst. I expect you did with your friends, too. Maybe because of your own fears. And you see, you've only ended up punishing yourself.'

'You're saying it's all my fault.' But I'm not arguing with her. She's right, obviously. Mothers always are.

'Don't be silly. It's no one's fault. You're wonderfully brave. Wonderfully loyal. No one is blaming anyone for anything.'

I blow my nose again. It's human nature to try to find someone to blame. Random bad things are especially hard to handle. Acts of God, we call them: blame the deity.

I sigh. 'And now I don't know what to do.'

'Get a good night's sleep,' my mother says, as if lifting it straight out of the *Good Mothering* manual.

'What about tomorrow?' I say.

'What about it?'

'Well . . . what will I do?'

'What you want to, I expect. There's not really a lot to decide, is there?'

I feel my mouth open. I want to wail *of course there is* and yet, even as I frame the wail, I sense the emptiness in the phrase. I can't back it with anything. My mother is reminding me that there is no escape. That nothing waits for you, or changes itself into something easier to handle, in your absence. You have to simply get on again. I know, already, that I will see and work with Francine again. Of course I will, if she'll still have me; that was acknowledged hours ago, when I envisaged telling her about me and Lionel. I already know that I will see Nick again; the alternative is unthinkable. I know that I care more about him than anyone else in the world. Even more than my mother. I'm just, at this particular moment, emotionally gridlocked.

'But I don't know if he's going to die or not. He still hasn't told me.'

My mother is silent. Then says, 'Why d'you think he wouldn't tell you the result over the phone?'

'He was angry. Upset. He wanted to hurt me.' I realize, suddenly, that I have not told her why. Not the whole of it. Not about Lionel. But my mother still understands. We have managed to make Lionel irrelevant.

'So what d'you think the result was? Based on that.'

My mother is trying to get me to say the unsayable. She waits a minute, and then says it herself.

'If he'd had bad news, wouldn't you suffer more if he'd told you? Why should he hide it? He wouldn't anyway, would he, darling? No one plays games with really bad news.'

I shake my head. I know she is right, but I mustn't be seen to be agreeing. I can let her words calm me inside but, outwardly, in case the fates are watching, I must look unconvinced.

She rises, pats my shoulder as if she understands how superstition operates and wouldn't dream of forcing me to tempt fate, and goes off to make hot drinks.

Horlicks is delicious. Why don't I drink this at home? Sweet and milky and wholesome. Liquid mothering. By the time I've finished I am almost serene. I am capable of undertaking non-stressful actions.

I have a couple of telephone calls to make. I'm not ready to speak to Nick yet and when I do it won't be over the phone, but I want him to know that I'm coming home. I ring the shop and leave a message on his answerphone. He won't get it till the morning, but that'll be soon enough. I say, 'This is Jessica. I'm staying over with Mum. I'll see you tomorrow. Today, when you hear this. Definitely. Goodnight.'

And then I ring Francine, because otherwise she'll wonder where I am tomorrow morning. She answers the phone herself and interrupts before I get the chance to tell her anything.

'Has Nick contacted you? He rang asking for the flat number.'

'Yes,' I say. 'We've spoken. I'm staying over with my mother tonight. In Reading.'

'Right.' Francine sounds abrupt, not her normal self. 'I trust the petition presentation went smoothly?'

'Yes,' I say. 'I'll tell you about it when I see you. There's lots to tell. But yes, it did.' Of course, Francine won't know what happened; we wouldn't have made the national news. Just the London region, if we were lucky. I can't face discussing the presentation now; it would mean discussing Lionel.

'Actually,' she says, sounding no keener than I to pursue the subject, 'I've a bone to pick with you.'

My grip tightens on the receiver. Christ, has Lionel spoken to her already?

'Why didn't you tell me? You must have known.'

'Sorry?' I make an effort of concentration. 'What are we talking about, Francine?'

I hear her take a deep breath. 'My friend Lydia gave me a lift home this evening after a meeting at her house. I'd asked Celia to collect me, but we finished early and Lydia offered. When I got home – unexpectedly, as I suppose Celia would see it – I found her and that lout who works in Nick's shop carrying on in the sitting room.'

'Lout?' I suddenly grasp who she means. 'Jason?'

'He's worse than that bloody Jonathan,' Francine complains. 'I don't know what's wrong with her.'

My brain is turning to soup. Celia and Jason. Of course. I'm an idiot. I absorb the information and immediately feel my loyalties torn. Francine sounds so vehement. But I must protect Jason. 'Oh, it's not that bad, surely.' I try to make light of it. 'He's a nice boy, Francine, honestly.'

'Don't be ridiculous. How can he be "nice"? Look at him. He's dirty.'

'No, he's not,' I say. 'The unshaven look is a fashion statement.' I don't attempt to justify his hair. I know Francine hates long hair on men.

'Why didn't you tell me?'

'I didn't know.'

'Come on.' Francine makes an exasperated noise. 'She says she's been seeing him for months.'

'I didn't know.' Because I was looking in the wrong direction, I add silently. I suddenly remember Celia coming in to my office to ask about Nick. No wonder she muddled me. Successfully distancing herself from Jason – *is he trustworthy?* – when the whole point – the only point – had been to ask his questions for him. All the time she was, indeed, keeping secrets; but I got the big secret wrong. So stupid – I even knew the type she liked: the ghastly Jonathan type.

'Nick must have known.'

'If he did, he didn't tell me. Perhaps he didn't want to put me in an awkward position. Perhaps Celia asked him not to. I've seen her at the shop, but that's all. I promise, Francine.' And there was that photo from the paper that Celia photocopied; because it showed Jason, of course, not Nick.

Francine makes a humphing sound. Grudging acceptance. Then says, 'Well, I'm very angry with her. They're obviously not suited. It'll be another disaster.'

'Mmm.' I try to sound non-committal. She's probably right. Bet it's Jason's heart that gets broken, though, not Celia's. And I bet Nick didn't know; or didn't acknowledge what he must have seen. He has been as dim – no, dimmer – than I. Neither of us, this last year, has been looking far beyond ourselves.

'I know you think these things aren't important, Jess, but she's my daughter, and I think they are . . .'

'I know. I know.' Will she be equally furious when she hears about me and Lionel? Her husband; still her husband. I have a feeling she might.

I say, 'I really rang to say that I'd like not to work

tomorrow. I'm dreadfully tired. I'd have to get up so early. D'you mind?'

'Of course not.' She sighs. 'I'm going to have a quiet day. You not here, and Celia not talking to me, because I called that boy a grubby yob.'

'To his face?'

'Don't be silly. Not to his bare backside either. No shame, honestly.'

'Oh God, Francine. They were . . .?'

'Quite. To the accompaniment of very loud music. Which is why they didn't hear me hobble in. I'm not feeling at all liberal-minded.'

'He'll apologize. If Celia tells him how upset you are.'

'I don't want his apologies. I want Celia to stop seeing him. But that, apparently, isn't going to happen.'

We end the phone call almost gossiping. I feel fraudulent, but tell myself I will be honest with her as soon as we meet face to face. I will.

I go to bed in the small cool spare back room where the bed is permanently made up. I nearly fall asleep immediately in a kind of reactive exhaustion, but just miss unconsciousness, and start to feel those structures inside me rebuilding. I wonder, not very seriously, if I should go for a run.

Eventually I have to get up to use the lavatory and,

walking back to the room, realize that my teeth are gritted. As if I'm angry.

I stop outside my door and think. If Nick's lump is malignant, what is he playing at, by not telling me? Hoping for a mortified reaction when I discover the truth? When I finally *come back to him* and discover it? When I'm forced to acknowledge that because of my bad behaviour, he's had to suffer the terrible truth alone?

No. It doesn't make sense. My mother is right. I would be suffering much more now if he had already told me. He would have, anyway; news like that would have overridden everything else.

So I am angry with him. Because I believe he is safe, but has kept the news from me. I know he has done this because he is angry too, and that he has a right to be angry. But that doesn't mean my rights are forfeit.

Anger with Nick is not the whole of it, though. I can detect more, a wide-flung splattering of fury. I am angry with doctors, hospitals, the entire system. I have learned things today about Nick's cancer that we should have known all year. That Nick's doctors should have told us. The unknown is always more terrifying than the known, and yet we have had to suffer it. Why, even if we didn't push the doctors to tell us the facts, didn't they tell us anyway? The onus, surely, is on them. They had the power, the knowledge; only they knew what we should be asking. We were ignorant. Nick was more than that: ill and ignorant. I was a mere visitor, not, apparently, their concern. And why, as the year progressed without recurrence, couldn't they have reassured us? Why couldn't they have simply told us what James told me today? What would be the harm – what could possibly be the harm, when the illness is cancer – in even over-optimistic reassurance? Whose well-being are they thinking of? Their own, in maintaining their cautious, professional reserve – and so being right, whatever the outcome – or ours? I feel cheated, as well as angry; precious time, precious peace of mind, has been stolen from us. I am angrier with them than I am with Nick.

I walk on to the bedroom and get back into bed. Naming my angers has inflamed them. My heart is pounding as if, instead of Horlicks, I have drunk a jug of coffee. I can feel thudding in the back of my head, through the pillow.

Footsteps patter in the corridor. The door opens and my mother comes in. She switches the side light on. She is wearing a pink double-layered nightie with a rosebud yoke that could have been Doris Day's, and carrying a glass of water.

'I can hear you are restless, dear,' she says. 'Have two of these.'

She hands me two capsules. I don't ask what they are; I trust her not to be poisoning me. After I've swallowed them and lain back, she strokes her hand across my forehead, as if checking for fever. The fact that I make this fever connection suggests that I am familiar with the gesture, that she must have caressed me like this when I was a child. Why do I only remember me looking after her?

Whatever the tablets are, they work. The scaffolding is dismantled again and the density of my flesh increases a thousand-fold. If I were a cartoon character I would be cutting a body imprint deep into the mattress. Before plummeting through on to the floor, I fall asleep.

Chapter 14

In the morning it is raining. Heavily and steadily. The sky is the colour of massed water, hundreds of thousands of gallons of it, suspended above the earth.

I have slept in till 8.30. My mother is already up and dressed and has put her face on. I hope that when I am sixty I look as youthful and ready to welcome the world at 8.30 in the morning. She organizes my breakfast; there is no frying pan in the house but she finds a packet of frozen croissants in the freezer and heats two up for me. I eat them with jam and wash them down with half a pint of milk.

My mother seems less maternal this morning. A male friend rings early and I have to listen to her fluttering over the phone at him, saying things like, 'You know me, Tommy, I'm so forgetful,' (this with a girlish giggle) and, 'You arrange it, darling, I'll only get in a muddle.' She is such a lazy person – why do they fall for it?

But she's still solicitous to me. She wants me to wait until the rain has eased before I leave and I rather agree, since motorways are so grim in the wet. However by eleven it is still raining and I can't wait any longer. I load the car and my mother kisses me goodbye, and I decide that if the sound of a cat purring is the world's most comforting sensory experience, the scent of face powder worn by women over sixty comes a close second.

The motorway, when I get on to it, is grim indeed. The two slower lanes are occupied by colossal lorries trailing plumes of rain-fog. Expensive cars with fat tyres and incompetent mudguards jet-spray my windscreen with filthy water as they hiss past at ninety miles an hour. There is nowhere for rain to go on the runway expanse of motorways, so it dances perpetually in the eight foot or so above the tarmac. As much seems to be rising as falling.

The far side of Swindon all traffic comes to a halt. Everyone panics in the slowdown, braking erratically and switching on their hazard warning lights. I am trapped in the middle lane and when we start to crawl again the differential movements of vehicles either side disorientate me. Nick would detest this. If he were on my left now – he would certainly not be driving – he would be turned away, staring out of the side window, the tension in his body willing the ordeal over. At intervals I would hear him blowing out air from his lungs, and I would know better than to speak to him and receive the snapping savagery of his anxiety.

We crawl for thirty minutes and then gradually pick up speed again. We pass no obvious hazards, no accident. Just a Mexican-wave jam, caused by the sheer volume of traffic. I stop at the next services for a break, intending to have a coffee and loosen my over-tense limbs, but hundreds of others, it seems, have the same idea. I have difficulty finding a parking space and even when I succeed and enter the service building, there are queues everywhere: at the toilets, the shop check-out, into the restaurant. Dozens of children and young men are playing the noisy arcade games that line the central hall, assaulting us with machine gun fire, or the scream of racing cars. In the occasional lulls piped muzac, fuzzy-sounding, as if it is being played through the building's air-conditioning system, takes over. There is a popcorn stall and chip counter by the entrance foyer and the air stinks of cooked chemicals. Everyone – including myself, I'm sure – looks appallingly overwrought and ugly. I leave the building and slam myself back in my car. Nick is right to loathe this sort of travel, I suddenly think. His phobia is not a neurosis; it is a sign of his uncorrupted sanity.

I exit from the motorway thirty miles further on and as I ascend the sliproad it's like leaving one climate and entering another. From the roundabout above I can look down and see the pall of road spray that hangs over the eight tarmac strips beneath. Up here it is simply raining.

By 1.30 I'm home, and parking the Golf behind my

flat. As I get out of the car there is a cloudburst with a roll of thunder, one of those vibrating, rumbling rolls, like Gargantuan furniture being moved overhead, and in the twenty-second run to the stairway my hair becomes plastered to my head. The wetness isn't cold though; I am sweating under my coat. And I am starting to feel sick. I was fine on the motorway; maybe the difficulties of the drive kept other feelings at bay.

I let myself into the flat, toss my case into the bedroom, and pick up the telephone. I need to know where Nick is. I ring the shop. Jason answers.

'Can I speak to Nick?'

Jason recognizes my voice. 'He's at home, Jess,' he says. 'He got your message. He's waiting for you.'

There's nothing ominous or overly significant in the way he says this. Nick hasn't confided in him. And of course Nick is right, we must meet on private ground.

I say, 'I hear Francine isn't very pleased with you and Celia.'

Jason says, 'Ah,' and gives an embarrassed laugh.

'She's not as fierce as she makes out,' I say. 'And not a prude. Just rather old-fashioned. She'd be impressed by an apology.'

'Really?' says Jason, doubtfully.

'Write it, if you like.' That's what people like Francine do. They write thank-you letters after parties, or house visits. Letters of sympathy. Letters of apology. Perhaps I should try it. This is a conversation I might be having with myself. 'She's into good manners,' I say.

I leave him to think about it. I don't bother to ring Nick to tell him I'm coming over; I can't as yet imagine our conversation, so I need him in front of me. That way, if we want, we can say nothing.

The rain outside is roaring. Below my window the High Street tarmac is white with bouncing water. I'm glad I'm not on the motorway now.

I can't find an umbrella. And I can't decide if I want anything to eat before I go. I feel I'm scattering, and in the end just grab my thin cotton jacket – what does it matter if I'm wet or hungry, for Christ's sake? – and leave.

Stepping out of the lobby downstairs is like stepping out under a full-on power-shower. Deluging, monsoon rain; in a different mood, on a different day, the sort of rain it would be worth getting into a swimsuit for. Inside the car I have to dry my hands on the passenger-seat upholstery before I can get a safe grip on the steering wheel. My windscreen seems to be leaking. Water is dripping on to my knee.

The main roads have become shallow, rushing rivers. One of the gutter storm drains has a small fountain above it as if water is being forced up through the grill, rather than draining into it. Further out of town leaves and twigs from overhanging trees have been beaten off their branches. I find myself thinking how clean everything will be after this.

Nick's Zodiac is in his driveway, when it should be in its garage. There will be a pool of water in the passenger footwell. I rush past to the shelter of the cottage porch and bang on the door. I think I hear music inside, above the din of the rain, but it may be my imagination. Whether it is or not, after I've banged, it stops.

The door opens and Nick stares at me. He says, 'You're very wet.'

The moment has come, and I don't know where to start. My crimes and his are all stored up inside me, but so intertwined I can't separate anything out. There is something on its own, though. The still-remaining edge of terror. I have to deal with that first.

I ask, 'Was the lump malignant or benign?'

Nick's face is unfriendly, but he's not going to lie to me.

'Benign,' he says. 'A lipoma. A fatty lump.'

I listen to the rain drumming behind me. 'Why were your lymph glands swollen?'

'Infection from the cat bite. I noticed my hand was stiff when I was playing at the Foundry. The consultant says it has to be that. They've given me antibiotics.'

I say, 'I spoke to a doctor yesterday. He said that if you hadn't had a recurrence by now, you were cured. And that malignant melanoma is such an aggressive cancer that if you weren't cured, you'd be dead by now.'

I watch movement in Nick's throat. Then he nods and says, 'At the hospital they said I was entitled to feel extremely optimistic.'

This is the first time since Nick's cancer was diagnosed that we have discussed his survival. No great triumph though; it's easy to discuss, now we're convincing ourselves he's safe. There is a moment's silence. Then he says, 'You'd better come in.'

I go through to the living room. He's been playing Muriel; she's out of her case and on the sofa. Terror is a strange emotion. When it disappears it leaves its shadow behind. You have to keep glancing back to check it's really gone.

I stand by the sofa and say the one thing I'm sure of. I say, 'I'm amazingly angry.'

'What?' Nick's tone is scornful, offensive. '*You're* angry?'

He is not upset – which he could have been. He, too, is angry. He can afford to be, since he is going to live. Anger has more stake in the future than grief.

'This conversation with a doctor,' he says. 'Was it before or after you slept with Lionel?'

Maybe he expects me to deny it. He can't know for sure.

'Had sex with him, you mean,' I say. 'After.'

He swings away, making a disgusted noise.

'I didn't know he was going to be there,' I say. 'Nothing was planned. He just turned up, and I used him.'

'For God's sake.'

'It was an act of rebellion. Against the cancer, not you. Just a defiance thing.'

'Francine be happy with this, will she?'

'I'm going to tell her. I expect she'll hate it. But I hope she'll understand.'

'Like I'm meant to?'

'Maybe.'

'Bitch.'

I know how seriously men take sexual infidelity – women's sexual infidelity, that is – but I had hoped Nick would be different. It looks like I'm wrong. This is the first time I have heard him call anyone – except a female dog – a bitch.

'It's not as cruel as you refusing to tell me the result of your biopsy,' I say.

'Since you hadn't deigned to come back, I assumed you didn't want to know.'

'Garbage. You were punishing me.'

'You deserve it. I had a hell of a day. I broke one of the bloody lights on the car, too, parking at the hospital.'

'Oh, that's my fault as well, is it? That you have such a large stupid car?'

'Could be, could be.'

'For Christ's sake.' The argument is becoming absurd. I suddenly wonder if I am missing something. I stare at Nick. He is genuinely furious, his face hard and tense. His flesh seems to shrink, or cling to the bones, in anger. But there is also something indiscriminate and unstoppable about his mood. I have it: he has no desire to be rational or reasonable or unridiculous. He is, quite simply, spoiling for a fight. And I am someone to fight with. This could be his moment. I feel myself respond, a fierce, hopeful aggression rising in me.

'I've had nobody this year,' I hiss. 'I'm entitled to go off the rails.'

'I see, I see. You've had nobody. Who d'you think I had?'

'You had me.'

'I had the fucking cancer too!' he shouts. 'You didn't.'

Nick hardly ever swears. I raise my voice to match. 'So? That wasn't my fault.'

'It wasn't mine either.'

'You kept threatening to change things. All that stupid magazine stuff.'

'So? So?'

'I don't want to be left.'

'Who said anything about leaving you?'

'You were, you were.' I am adamant. I am right. I was threatened. I was holding his cancer for him, while he was trying to leave it behind. I couldn't, daren't, let it go. Someone had to hold it.

'So because you were scared of me leaving you, you bugger off to London and screw Lionel? That's very logical.'

He is sneering at me. I want to hit him. Get my hands on him. I'm fed up with words. The real target has disappeared but I can get close. His bad leg. Except, of course, it isn't bad any more.

I kick him on the knee, hard. It's as high as I can get.

'Jesus, shit!' He grabs at himself 'Jess!'

I make a fist. His expression is outraged, insufferably outraged. I swing at his left cheekbone but he is too quick and slaps my arm away. He grabs the front of my sodden jacket, twists the material in his hand, and jerks me towards him. I hear something crack. It might be the material, but it might also be the barrier, the glass wall between us. His face is less than six inches from mine. I can feel his anger and for a moment I am frightened, because it is real, hot anger, not the encouraging, cooperative aggression I am used to. But then with his free hand he moves Muriel out of the way, so she won't get damaged, and I know he still has self-control. My fear dies.

We fight like we haven't for more than a year. In our fights we do not punch or bite or scratch, but we do wrestle and push, even kick, if there is space between us to swing a leg. To be reckless with your body – it's the great freedom, the prerogative of the young and healthy. We've only once really hurt ourselves, when the work table in my sitting room collapsed under us, and then it was Nick's forehead that hit the corner of the wooden chair seat, not mine. We keep away from hard objects and fireplaces, usually. I get the better deal because Nick is so much heavier and stronger than I am, and so he has to be more careful. I can give all I've got.

Of course Nick always wins. No, that's the wrong word. We both win. But physically he overwhelms me. The fact that I, too, count this as a win has nothing to do with a liking for helplessness on my part, nothing at all. Quite the contrary: it's my passion for strength. What's his is mine. But they don't show it unless you make them.

And there's nothing like the strength of a man who's going to live. We have decided that he is going to live. He could be hit by a sludge tanker tomorrow. The cancer might still be inside him, the slow, unaggressive exception that proves the rule. It might come back. A meteorite could fall on the cottage and kill us both right now. But we're not going to live our lives in the expectation or fear of it. We are making our decision and maybe we're even lucky, because we can do this earlier than most. We're drawing our finish line, now.

When we've finished drawing it I'm on my back on the floor, and Nick is kneeling over me, and releasing me. We have fought to a standstill – accurately, a lie-still – and I have called – gasped – a halt. The air is noisy with our breathing. My wrists burn. I will have finger bruises on my arms, and I expect Nick will too. A kick bruise on his knee, definitely. Two upright chairs with padded seats got knocked over and lying like this I can see their webbing innards; when Nick re-upholstered them he must have left the hessian covering off. I feel his forehead push against my shoulder as he slumps down to my side, and he has enough energy left to groan in my ear.

I feel as if we have made love, though we haven't. Sometimes we do, after a fight, sometimes we don't. It depends on Nick's mood, on why we have fought. He can find my aggression arousing, but not his own. So this occasion is not one for lovemaking. Although he has relieved his feelings this doesn't mean his anger has disappeared. But he is less angry than he was. I can feel it. The worst is over.

I lift my head and peer down at my front. 'You've torn the zip on my jacket.' The metal teeth look undamaged, but half the material strip on the right has been ripped from its seam.

'Tough.'

Nick's tone is ungiving, but normally so. Recognizably so. A resentful tone I have heard many times. Perhaps not this last year, but before. I smile to myself. Bet I can get him to mend the zip. He's good with the sewing machine.

He turns his face into my shoulder and says, grudgingly, 'Since you're here, I've something to show you.'

'Oh yes?'

'In a minute.'

We wait a minute, almost companionably now it seems, gathering breath. I am so tired, so peacefully tired, that I close my eyes. When the minute has passed

I feel Nick's weight leave my shoulder, as he hauls himself up. I know that he is fully clothed but in my mind's eye, behind my closed lids, I see him naked. I see the thin line down his thigh, silver-white now. The wider one above his groin, still pink, but acquiring the sheen that says *old scar*. I see his perfect, imperfect body, that he shares only with me. I am sorry that I shared mine with Lionel. Truly sorry; I could apologize for it now. I wonder if Nick'll let me stay here tonight? Or is it too soon? The kitchen door creaks, opening and closing. There are a few seconds of silence. Then another creak, as Nick returns.

Something lands on my stomach. I open my eyes and I am staring into the tiny, blue-eyed face of a tabby kitten. Fuzzy yellow-and-grey ears. Bumble-bee striped legs, braced from the fall. Minute transparent claws grip the cotton waistband of my trousers. As I lift my hand to touch the kitten's head, its mouth opens in a pink, needle-toothed baby roar.

CATHERINE MERRIMAN

State of Desire

£6.99

'Whatever the danger, whatever the hurt to others, the state of desire is all-consuming . . .'

Jenny Parsons' husband died suddenly a year ago; she is only just starting to rediscover herself. Now though, the mountain behind her house in South Wales is threatened by a vast mining operation. Jenny is distraught and, encouraged by her friend Sal, channels her resurfaced strength into trying to save the mountain.

But her energy spills over, suddenly and uncontrollably, into a reckless affair with one of her son's friends. Mark is only twenty-five, fourteen years Jenny's junior; the liaison is foolhardy, fraught with misunderstandings. But Jenny is being driven by deep, inexplicable passions. She is convinced that, through Mark, she can reclaim some part of herself, a part she'd thought lost with Michael's death . . .

'Catherine Merriman brings a bold, bruised sensuality to this wry chronicle of life beyond bereavement'
She

CATHERINE MERRIMAN

Fatal Observations

£5.99

Jane Hardy, thirty-six and unmarried, lives alone in a mansion block in North London. Untaxed by her job as a college lecturer, and bored by her undemanding relationship with her boyfriend, things begin to look up when tenants move into the flat downstairs, and the even tenor of her life is shaken.

Ruth and Harry are an odd and unlikely couple, she a career solicitor, he a leather-clad biker, but soon they become Jane's close companions. Harry in particular turns out to be fiercely loyal, and very protective when Jane is besieged by visits from a friend's violent ex-husband.

When the police can do nothing to intervene, Harry the frustrated man of action, opts for his own brave but foolhardy brand of rough justice . . . with horrific consequences . . .

'Tense, sinister, shocking'
Woman's Journal

CATHERINE MERRIMAN

Leaving the Light On

£5.99

Winner of the Ruth Hadden Memorial Award

Retreating from a broken and bitter relationship, Barbara just wants to have some fun and not think too hard about anything. So when she moves to a new town and a new job, the group of ready-made friends she's introduced to by a colleague seems perfect.

But as Barbara gets to know them better, she finds that their behaviour demands much closer scrutiny. Why does Sonia sleep with Len when he obviously despises her? Why is Len so cruel to Billy when he's supposed to be his friend? Why does Billy accept this cruelty as though it's all he deserves? Barbara would rather not know, but as the summer wears on the tension mounts and Barbara finds herself caught up in a terrifying power game, which she soon realizes isn't a game at all . . .

'Catherine Merriman studs every page with little jewels of insight and humour'
Western Mail